The door to Jeff's apartment was locked. Tom began pounding on the door but when there was no answer to his calls to Jeff, he tried breaking it open with his shoulder. Then a man in a robe came up with a key and said he was the building custodian.

Tom entered the apartment with two young paramedics. They found a girl face-down on the couch, her right arm hanging limp to the floor. Tom saw Jeff slumped in an easy chair, his head fallen to his chest. An open, empty bottle of pills lay on the floor nearby.

Other Tom Delos and the Guardians adventures:

UP FROM NOWHERE
ONE-WAY TRIP
EASY WAY OUT

THE FINAL ACT

WALTER OLEKSY

A TOM DELOS
AND THE
GUARDIANS
ADVENTURE
#4

TEMPO BOOKS, NEW YORK

All characters in this book are fictitious.
Any resemblance to actual persons, living or dead,
is purely coincidental.

THE FINAL ACT

A Tempo Book/published by arrangement with
the author

PRINTING HISTORY
Tempo Original/February 1984

All rights reserved.
Copyright © 1984 by Walter Oleksy
This book may not be reproduced in whole
or in part, by mimeograph or any other means,
without permission. For information address:
The Berkley Publishing Group,
200 Madison Avenue, New York, N.Y. 10016

ISBN: 0-441-23530-1

Tempo Books are published by The Berkley Publishing Group,
200 Madison Avenue, New York, New York 10016.
Tempo Books are registered in the United States Patent Office.
PRINTED IN THE UNITED STATES OF AMERICA

THE FINAL ACT

1

Tom Delos took the left jab to the side of his head. Stumbling backward, he caught a hard right on the other side, spun around, and fell face-down on the canvas. Trying to lift himself up on rubbery arms, the tall, muscularly built seventeen-year-old heard the referee start counting over him.

"One. Two. Three. Four. . . ."

"Stay down till eight," Tom heard his coach call out over the roaring and shouting in the gym.

". . . Five. Six. Seven. . . ."

Was that the bell? Tom wasn't sure, over the crowd noise, and he managed to get to his knees. Next thing he knew, his coach and second were grabbing him under the arms and half-dragging him to his corner.

Tom refused to sit on his stool to rest between rounds, breathing hard as he leaned cockily back against the ropes in his corner. "They were lucky punches," he said, after his coach, Johnny Lynch, took out his mouthpiece.

"You've got to win round three or it's all over," the gray-haired, barrel-chested man said, toweling perspiration and blood off his young boxer's handsome face. Tom's thick black hair fell wet over his forehead and covered a cut over his left eye.

Tom's best friend, Jimmy Ryan, a good-looking, sandy-haired boy his age, pulled down the front of the waistband of Tom's white satin boxing trunks and began massaging his midsection. "Didn't we warn you to block his left?"

"It was his right that sent me down," Tom groused, tossing his head back to get the hair out of his eyes.

"It was the left that set you up," his coach advised. "And you ought to know by now, Cas Stanwyck don't have any 'lucky' punches. He's the coolest fighter I've seen in years. Not the best, but the coolest."

"I'm on fire," Tom said, and asked for water with which to wash his mouth out. Jimmy gave him a drink and Tom spat it into a pail. "I'll cool him off. He's been after me long enough. Now's my chance to deck him and I'm gonna do it, this round."

Jimmy poured water over Tom's shoulders and chest. The crowd was loving it, seeing Tom standing arrogantly while Cas sat. He could hear his own rooting section clapping and whistling for him. Maury and Scotty and the other Guardians were in the bleachers just below the ring, sitting with Tom's girlfriend and sister. Just about everybody he knew was there, cheering for him. How could he let them down? He didn't intend to.

Jimmy climbed through the ropes and stood behind Tom on the skirt of the ring, massaging his shoulders. Johnny Lynch gave Tom a final word of encouragement, patted the front of his trunks to check his supporter, and climbed out of the ring just as the bell clanged.

Tom came out of his corner like a charging bull for the

THE FINAL ACT

third and final round. It was only an exhibition bout between rival Chicago Park district boxing clubs, but a grudge fight to Tom. He and Cas Stanwyck were both light-heavyweights, but Tom at 170 pounds was about eight pounds lighter than red-haired Cas. Cas was eighteen, almost a year older than Tom, and bigger, with a longer reach.

None of it mattered to Tom. Cas had been playing tough guy and bigshot ever since they'd met about a year before, beating Tom every time they had been paired off against each other. Tom decided it was now or never. He began landing some good blows to Cas's chest and midsection, remembering what his coach had told him: "You don't have to knock a guy out to win. Just land more punches."

But Tom knew Cas didn't fight that way. He didn't hit as often. His strategy was to land a knockout punch.

Tom's arms were so tired, his gloves felt like they were set in concrete. He no longer hoped to knock Cas out. But if he did what his coach said and landed more punches, maybe he could still win on points.

Tom knew that Cas was no dummy. He'd figured out Tom's strategy of winning on points and had given up doing the same himself. The more Tom landed punches to the body, the more Cas tried for a knockout punch, with as many low blows in between as the referee would let him get away with.

One low blow sent Tom doubling up, nearly onto his knees. The referee warned Cas that another such blow would cost him the round, but the warning didn't faze Cas. He came on strong as ever with body punches and swings and uppercuts that Tom managed to dodge.

Tom took another hard left to the head. It made him fall back, but he was able to duck the right that followed. Crouching low, Tom went after Cas's midsection and began landing some good blows that sent the bigger fighter back against the ropes. Not only Tom's cheering section but most of the rest of the spectators in the small, steamy gym got to their feet, yelling for Tom to put Cas away.

After the referee broke them up, Cas swung a hard right at Tom's face, but Tom ducked again. He drove in once again for more shots at the body until Cas's knees buckled and he fell backward against the ropes.

Tom could hardly believe it. The big moose of a guy was caving in!

Again the referee sent Tom to a neutral corner and began counting over Cas, then gave up and looked into his eyes.

"That's it," the ref called out to the judges at ringside. "Fight's over."

A moment later, Tom felt his right arm get lifted into the air and heard the referee announce that he'd won the fight by a technical knockout. It was more than he'd hoped for.

Jimmy climbed into the ring and grabbed Tom around the waist, spinning him around happily. Johnny Lynch came over with Tom's boxing robe, putting it over his fighter's shoulders. The robe was blue satin with the name, The Guardians, sewn on the back in silver script lettering.

Tom never felt better in his life than he did that moment in the Turner Park gym ring, his best friend hugging him and everyone else standing up at ringside, cheering their heads off. The referee made it official, naming him the winner of the light-heavyweight division of the park district matches. Tom wished his mother could have been there, and his father, too. He'd finally made something of himself; he was a champion, and it felt so good. But they weren't there to see it.

Tom felt as if he'd walked a thousand miles or fought ten thousand hours in the span of the three two-minute rounds and the moment of victory. He'd put his whole life into those three rounds. It had all seemed over, and for nothing, when he was lying flat on his face on the canvas. The bell had saved him and he had a chance to get his energy back and think over how much he wanted to win. It was more than just another fight, and more than even a grudge match against Cas. It was as if Tom knew he wouldn't have any future if he didn't win that fight. Feeling like that, he knew he had to win.

Now I can really start to put things behind me, he thought as he stood in the middle of the ring with everyone yelling at him that he'd won, and he remembered it all. In waves, faces and things that had happened to him for years all came back. The street fights to survive in the roughest neighborhoods of Chicago. Fighting back when they laughed at him because his father was in prison for drug trafficking, and his mother had taken to the streets. All the hard times he'd endured worrying that his kid sister, Ellie, was becoming like her mother. His best friend then, Larry Schroeder, a handsome blond kid he'd hero-worshipped, getting blown apart by shotgun blasts in an aborted drug deal that backfired. The nut who set it up, a kid named Angel, setting fire to the building Tom's mother and sister lived in, then getting trapped in the basement and the building falling in on him.

Tom remembered the day about a year before when he went before a lady judge on a botched-up robbery charge and got put on probation. His probation officer, Paul Maggiore, found a loft in a warehouse for Tom to live in, and Tom put in with five other guys like himself, kids with lousy pasts and doubtful futures, trying to make a better life for themselves by pulling together, calling themselves the Guardians. They would guard each other against pimps and pushers and anyone else who tried to use them or take advantage of them. By themselves, they might not make it. Together, they all had a chance.

His father had been killed in prison. His mother had just died after being hit by a car driven by a wild kid who had had too much to drink and was pursued by boozed-up punk rockers.

He didn't want to think about any of it and all the rest that tried to flash itself in front of his mind like one long, bad dream. He danced up and down in the middle of the ring as Johnny Lynch took out his mouthpiece and Jimmy began untying his gloves, looking down to see the faces that were alive and meant everything to him. The other Guardians—Maury, Scotty, Midget, and Wyllis. And, of course, Jimmy, standing in front of him as his robe fell to the canvas.

He'd won the fight as much for Jimmy as he had for himself. Jimmy could never fight again. He had nearly been killed when punk rockers had hit him on the head in an alley fight. He survived the concussion, but medics warned he'd be risking his life if he went back into the ring. Instead, Jimmy declared he'd second Tom and help train him for next year's Golden Gloves bouts and, after that, maybe even the Olympics or professional boxing.

Tom saw his girl, Marty, at ringside with his sister. Marty was going to make it in gymnastics, the way Tom was going to make it in boxing. They had a future together, too; he felt it stronger then than he had felt anything before. They'd make a life for themselves, but not too soon. Not until they both had a few more years to work and grow and know each other and know what life was all about. His mother had warned him and Ellie enough against marrying too young. "Give yourself a chance to live, before you tie yourself down with all the responsibilities of marriage." She had warned him so often he knew it by heart.

What was the hurry, anyway, to get married or even to get too serious? He'd been in a hurry all his life and it had been getting him nowhere fast. Now, thanks to his friends and Paul Maggiore, Tom had slowed down a little. He'd taken time to think things out and to look around and see where he was going. He was still only seventeen. What *was* the hurry, anyway, about anything? And he wanted to savor the moment, the victory, and make it last a lifetime.

Jimmy put Tom's robe back over his shoulders and began massaging him when Tom remembered Cas Stanwyck and went across the ring to check on him. Cas's handlers were working on him as he sat on his stool in his corner when Tom came up to him.

"Are you all right, Cas?" Tom asked.

Cas glared at Tom and threw out a gloved hand to push him away.

"Hey, let's shake and forget it, okay?" Tom asked, extending a hand.

Cas got to his feet shakily and began to climb out of the ring, leaving Tom to look after him, shaking his head.

A big, black boxer began climbing into the ring for the next bout, a heavyweight match, and Tom followed Cas out of the ring. His friends and Marty and Ellie hurried over to congratulate him, and Tom saw Paul Maggiore and Bernie Schmidt with them. Bernie was Tom's and Jimmy's boss. He owned a construction business and they were on his remodeling crew, tearing down old houses and helping build new ones. Tom liked the work a lot and put the pay to good use, buying Paul's old Volkswagen and fixing up the loft for himself and the other Guardians.

It had been prearranged that, win or lose, they'd all get together after the fight and celebrate at The Hot Spot, a pizzeria that was also their hangout.

Jimmy led the way to the shower room and Tom liked it when people he didn't even know reached out from the seats and congratulated him as he walked up the aisle to the back of the gym. *So this is how it feels*, he thought, *to be a winner*. He liked it a lot.

He expected to see Cas Stanwyck in the shower but he

wasn't there. Afterward, toweling himself dry in the locker room, and not seeing him there, either, Tom decided that Cas had just split, sweat and all, as soon as he lost. Well, he'd tried; he'd offered a hand in friendship to Cas. If he didn't take it, that was Cas's decision. Maybe somewhere down the line they could still bury whatever was bugging Cas. Now all Tom could think of was how good the shower felt, the hot water falling on a winner this time.

Standing in his boxer shorts in the locker room, after drying off from the shower, Tom impulsively gave Jimmy a hug.

"That's for being in my corner, always," Tom said emotionally. He'd never been one to express emotion, especially toward another guy. But Jimmy Ryan was special and Tom told him so. He was a special person and a special friend.

Self-consciously, Jimmy said the feeling was mutual and hugged Tom back.

"It's been good, Tom," the good-looking, sandy-haired boy said. "Knowing you, being a Guardian. I didn't have much, before. Now I feel like I've got a home and a family."

Jimmy, orphaned at ten and living in orphanages, foster homes, and institutions until he was seventeen, had met Tom and joined the Guardians, and had become like a brother to Tom. Tom approved that Jimmy and Ellie were dating and that things were good between them. They weren't in a hurry to get serious, either. The four of them had great times together and Tom hoped it could go on like that forever.

But he sensed that something was bothering his best friend. Maybe it was because Jimmy wished he'd been able to fight that night. It was the first boxing match Jimmy had been to in which he couldn't put on the gloves and had to work, instead, in Tom's corner. Tom wouldn't ask about it. If that was it, he'd let Jimmy alone and would understand.

After Tom dressed, they went back out and viewed the

heavyweight fight, watching two big black guys battle it out. Tom was glad he wasn't in the ring with either of them.

Afterward they piled in Tom's and Paul's cars and drove to The Hot Spot about a mile north of the gym in the Belmont Harbor neighborhood where the Guardians lived. The owner, Luigi Carmen, an old friend of theirs, had reserved a big round corner table for them.

"Where's Bernie?" Tom asked as they all sat at the table and began deciding what kind of pizzas to order.

Tom again saw a troubled look on Jimmy's face.

"He said he was sorry but he couldn't join us," Jimmy said as casually as he could.

Jimmy wasn't fooling Tom; something was wrong. Tom didn't like the idea of anything spoiling his night for him, but it wasn't like Jimmy to hold anything back from him. If there was some kind of trouble, and Jimmy or Bernie were involved, Tom had to know about it.

"What's going on?" Tom persisted, looking across the table at Jimmy.

Tom felt Marty put her hand on his. She looked prettier than ever, in a dark blue sweater and jeans, her long auburn hair looking so soft he wanted to touch it. She was nearly Tom's age—she had recently turned seventeen and he was getting close to eighteen.

"Let it go until tomorrow," Marty said to Tom. "Enjoy tonight."

Something *was* going on. Tom had to know what it was. He didn't like secrets or being left out when things were going good *or* bad. It was something he'd tried to get across to all his friends, that talking things out and bringing problems into the open was the only way they could help each other. Now everyone at the table except him seemed to know that something was going on. And unless he was badly mistaken, it wasn't anything good.

"All right, Jimmy," Tom said, getting up. "Let's go somewhere and talk."

Jimmy got up grudgingly and followed as Tom walked over to the video games in an adjoining room.

"Now what's it all about?" Tom asked his friend. "Lay it on me. I know it's got to be some kind of bad news."

"I didn't want to tell you until tomorrow," Jimmy said as if dreading to be the bearer of bad news. "It's something Bernie told me tonight, before your bout."

Tom became worried. "His kid's all right, isn't he?" Tom was afraid Bernie's newborn son had become ill. They had all been at the infant's christening only about a month before.

"No, it isn't Alex," Jimmy said, putting a hand on Tom's shoulder. "It's just this rotten economy. Bernie's having trouble meeting his payroll. Some new work he thought he'd had lined up fell through. He's got to cut back on his crew."

Tom got the picture. Jimmy didn't have to say more.

"So he's got to lay us off," Tom said. "Both of us?"

Jimmy nodded. "He said that as soon as he can, he'll rehire us. He likes us and he likes our work; it's just that he has no other choice. He's got to pick us to let go because we were the last guys he hired. He owes it to the other guys who have been with him longer to keep them on, as long as he can. And they're older anyway and some have kids."

It was just about the worst news Tom could have gotten. He was depending on his job to learn a trade and to make money.

"Did he think it would be for long?" Tom asked anxiously. "A few weeks or a month or what?"

"He said not to count on him rehiring us, if we found something else," Jimmy said. "It might be a long time before things pick up and he could put us back on."

But jobs are scarce as hell, Tom was thinking. Everybody's out of work, especially unskilled young guys like him

THE FINAL ACT 11

and Jimmy. He knew guys their age who hadn't worked in over a year. And he and Jimmy weren't eligible for unemployment compensation. Bernie hadn't hired them full time and they hadn't paid into unemployment compensation to get anything back from it.

Seeing how badly Jimmy felt, having to be the bearer of Bernie's bad news, Tom tried to laugh it off.

"Well, what the hell," Tom said with a shrug. "If everybody's out of work, at least we won't be alone."

He put an arm around his friend's shoulder and they walked back to the table to rejoin the party. He could tell that they all knew the news already. *At least that was a break,* Tom thought.

"Okay, what'll it be?" Tom asked his friends as he took his seat again next to Marty, and Jimmy went back to sit beside Ellie. "Sausage? Anchovies? Green pepper? Mushrooms?"

"It's my treat," Paul Maggiore spoke up. "Order the works!"

Tom looked across the table at his friend the probation officer, a thickly built man in his late thirties, with thinning brown hair streaked with gray. *A nice guy, despite his occupation,* Tom was thinking.

"Like hell it's your treat!" Tom exclaimed. "Who won tonight, anyway?"

2

Tom didn't mind the first few days of being out of work. He enjoyed the luxury of sleeping late and goofing off with Jimmy. Spring had come on early and strong. Everything was green and Tom and Jimmy and sometimes some of the other guys drove around the city and checked things out.

After the third day, though, Jimmy began to get anxious about finding another job. The man who owned the warehouse, Mitchell Kowalski, let the Guardians live in the loft rent-free and even agreed to pay the gas, electric, and phone bills, as a favor to Paul Maggiore. Paul had tried to help Kowalski's teenage son Danny when he was on drugs, but the boy had died. Helping Tom and his pals with a place to live was Kowalski's way of trying to make it up to Danny.

But even without those bills to worry about, Jimmy had to think about food and money for other things they'd need to live on. What if one of them got sick? They didn't have insurance to cover any hospital bills that might come up. And Tom needed money for the car, not only for gas, but for more repair work as well. He did most of it himself, with Jimmy and Maury helping when he needed it. But parts cost money, and it was an old VW, rusting to death.

Maury had a job at a gas station. He wanted to be helpful, but when he suggested Tom drive over while the station owner was on lunch break and he'd fill the gas tank for him free, Tom objected. He insisted he wasn't desperate enough to take handouts, even if they were legal. He wished Maury hadn't even suggested it.

Scotty had an after-school job bagging groceries in a Latino grocery store a few blocks from the warehouse. Midget and Wyllis had after-school jobs at a news delivery agency. None of them made much but it brought in something to the Guardians' common finances.

Jimmy had graduated from high school while living in an orphanage. Tom and Maury had both dropped out of school in their senior years. At first, after he'd lost his job, Tom thought of going back to school and getting his high school diploma. But the idea of going to school instead of working and earning money didn't appeal to him. Maybe after he'd found a new full-time job he'd go to night school to finish up. He put it in the back of his mind while he and Jimmy looked for work, making the rounds of factories in the neighborhood.

Nobody was hiring. In front of every place they went, they stared at signs saying NO HELP WANTED.

They tried the unemployment office in the neighborhood, but the few jobs offered there were for computer operators or accountants or other skilled workers. The fact that he wasn't eligible for the only jobs available began to bug Tom. He emphasized that he knew carpentry skills, but the clerk in the unemployment office shrugged that off and said the building trade was just not hiring. Later, after the economy picked up, construction jobs would be available, but not now.

THE FINAL ACT

Before Tom knew it, a week had gone by. He hadn't given up yet, and he checked the want ads in the newspaper every day, but he didn't find anything for him or for Jimmy. He even put up cards in the neighborhood supermarkets offering to repair cars; anything to earn some money. But no one called.

By the end of the second week, Tom was almost coming unglued. He couldn't sleep at night, his temper grew shorter, and he found himself arguing with the other guys. He and Maury got into it a couple of times, about such little things that Tom couldn't even remember what brought the arguments on afterward. He even laced into Jimmy once, when Jimmy borrowed one of his shirts. It was a yellow silk shirt that had belonged to Tom's once best friend, Larry Schroeder, and Tom had kept it to sort of keep his friend alive for him after he'd been killed in the aborted drug bust almost a year before. He made Jimmy take off the shirt and then told him in no uncertain terms that he wasn't to wear that particular shirt ever again. But afterward, Tom didn't put on the shirt himself, either. Instead, he crumpled it into a ball, threw it onto his bed, and stormed out of the warehouse.

He went into the alley behind the warehouse and decided to throw his nervous energy into adjusting the carburetor in his car. It had been knocking lately. While Tom was working on the car, Jimmy came up to him and began making small talk. Tom picked up on it right away, glad his friend knew him so well. They didn't have to apologize to each other for anything, ever. They just went back to being best friends again without anything said.

When Tom had the carburetor working to his satisfaction, he suggested he and Jimmy take a ride to Belmont Harbor and check out the yachts in the lagoon. It was one of Tom's favorite places. He dreamed of being rich one day and owning a yacht that he'd have moored there. He'd take the Guardians and Marty and his sister way up Lake Michigan to Mackinac Island in northern Michigan.

Tom drove east on Belmont Avenue and parked the car in a lot near the Chicago Yacht Club, among much newer and more expensive car that belonged to members who owned the boats in the harbor. They got out and walked along the bike path beside the water, and Tom dreamed again about owning a boat like the ones bobbing gently in the lagoon.

After a while, his attention was drawn to two men he saw nearby, leaning on a railing overlooking the harbor. He didn't recognize them, but suspected he knew what they were doing there. One of the men, wearing a tan suit, was older and bigger. The other looked about Tom's age, and was in jeans and casually dressed.

Tom nudged Jimmy and they watched as a third man, in white slacks and sportcoat, approached the other two at the railing. That man reached into an inside coat pocket and handed something to the man in the tan suit and got an envelope in exchange.

Tom didn't have to tell Jimmy what it was; Jimmy could see that it was a drug deal. The guy who had just come up was a dealer. He was gone as fast as he'd come, and the other guys began walking toward Tom and Jimmy, heading for the lot where Tom's car was parked.

As the men approached him, Tom became aware that he knew one of them, Earl Mabley, a two-bit drug trafficker with whom Tom had had the misfortune of getting involved the previous fall. Mabley had been driving a car used in a phony videotape racket that was used as a front for pushing "look-alike" drugs. The capsules resembled speed but were really look-alikes, heavy doses of impure drugs that gave kids a bad trip. Some kids had even died. Tom had helped Paul Maggiore break up the racket, after Tom's girl, Marty,

THE FINAL ACT

had nearly died of the stuff when someone pushed some of it on her. Tom thought a judge had put Mabley away for a while. Now he figured Mabley had gotten off on probation or was out on bail. He could see the man was back doing business as usual.

Mabley recognized Tom and started walking toward him. He still reminded Tom of a wrestler, a bull-sized man with thinning brown hair, his white-shirted stomach hanging out over the belt of his flashy tan slacks. Tom couldn't help but feel apprehensive, since only a few months before he'd put the finger on Mabley and his pal, Tony Costello, who had been a cop on the take.

He didn't recognize the guy with the drug trafficker. He reminded Tom of someone, but he couldn't think who, someone he'd seen somewhere but didn't know. He was a good-looking kid of maybe seventeen, not really tall, but with a good build, like a gymnast's or swimmer's, and his blond hair was tightly curled. Then Tom realized who the boy reminded him of—Chris Atkins, the movie star from *The Blue Lagoon*. But he wasn't wearing a loincloth; he was in Levi's and an expensive-looking tan suede vest. *With the red satin cowboy shirt he wore under the vest, and the pointed brown boots*, Tom thought, nearly laughing, *all he needed was the ten-gallon hat and a horse*.

"Look," Mabley said to the young man he was with, stopping just as they came up to Tom and Jimmy. "An old friend of mine. Delos, ain't it? Tom Delos?"

Tom knew the big goon knew his name well enough. He was playing a game of cat and mouse. Tom knew who the mouse was, but figured he could handle the fat cat any day. Mabley might be trouble, but he was basically a loser. Tom had handled him before, he could handle him again.

Mabley reached out a hand. Surprised, Tom took it.

"Hey, no hard feelings, Tommy," Mabley said out of the

side of his mouth. His nose was flat, like a pug's, and it didn't help the rest of his looks. "How're tricks?"

"Swell," Tom shot back. "Couldn't be better."

Mabley looked him over. "You working?" he asked.

Tom tried to think of something fast. "Sure. Working in a friend's construction business."

Mabley could see through him. "Not much going on in that line lately. Hey, if you're out of work and need some money, I know how you can get some. Easy work, good hours, great pay."

Tom could guess doing what. Pushing more look-alikes, or working in some other drug-related racket Mabley was into. He figured the cowboy was in on it with him. He had to be, if he was there when a deal was being made.

"This here kid knows his way around," Mabley said confidentially to the cowboy. "He could do well for himself, if he was smart. But some probation officer got to him."

Tom could feel the cutting edge of Mabley's attitude toward him. If they weren't in a public place, in broad daylight, he figured Mabley wouldn't hesitate to pull a gun or knife on him. Mabley sure owed Tom one, for breaking up the look-alike racket and putting him before a judge. But Tom remembered the judge had given Mabley ten years for his part in the drug racket. He wondered how Mabley was back out on the streets so fast. On an appeal, he figured. Chicago hoods never went to prison; they always managed to get out on the street for years while they appealed their convictions, then they never seemed to be put away. They had enough money and knew the right lawyers, or the right judges, too, for that matter. He knew Mabley had some connections pretty high up. He'd probably gotten out on bond while his case was being appealed, then laid low for the winter in the Florida sunshine, and now was back doing business as usual. He wondered if Costello was, too? Cos-

THE FINAL ACT

tello would really be out to get him, because Tom had exposed him as a crooked narcotics detective and had gotten him kicked off the police force.

Tom didn't care. He wouldn't mind trading punches with Mabley or Costello, or the cowboy for that matter. He still felt he didn't do enough to Mabley and Costello, to get back at them for nearly killing Marty. He could handle them. He didn't even worry that they might bump him off, like they had Phil Beasley, a go-between with whom they had worked the videotape look-alike racket. When Phil held back some payoff money from them, they had him shot and had stuffed his body in the trunk of a car. Tom wouldn't give them a chance to do the same to him, he decided, as he stood looking at Mabley in Belmont Harbor.

"I told you, Tom," Mabley reminded, putting a hand on Tom's shoulder, "no hard feelings. Tony and I talked it over afterward and agreed. You're like one of us. We grew up just like you. We know what it's like, to be a street kid in Chicago."

Tom figured that was true enough. Only Costello hadn't seen what Tom had. Tom was well on his way to becoming jail bait or worse, when one morning about a year before, he'd seen Larry Schroeder get his stomach and half his face blown away by shotgun blasts. The blasts had been intended for Tom, but the gunmen had gotten them mixed up and Larry got it instead. Seeing Larry lying dead in a pool of blood shook Tom out of it. If he kept on going as he was, he'd wind up just like Larry. Thanks to that and his probation officer Paul Maggiore, Tom began to pull himself into a smarter direction and got some other kids like himself to put in together and form the Guardians.

Mabley took out his wallet and tried to press some green folding money onto Tom. "You look like you could use some," he said, but Tom refused. *Maybe it was marked,*

Tom thought. Mabley would like nothing better than to plant some marked money on Tom, for cops to find. Then some judge on their payroll would put Tom away for good.

"If you need work, you know who to come to," Mabley offered.

"I'm okay," Tom shot back.

"Okay," Mabley said, putting his money away. "Come on, kid. Steak and eggs for lunch? Maybe some wine, too? These guys don't know how to take a favor when it's offered."

Mabley put a hand around his young friend's waist and started to walk toward the parking lot. Tom could see that the boy didn't go for Mabley putting his hands on him, but he didn't push them off. After a few steps, Mabley looked over his shoulder.

"I'll be seeing you around," Mabley said. "If you change your mind, let me know."

"What was that all about?" Tom heard the cowboy ask as Mabley began walking on again.

Tom figured Mabley would tell the baby-faced kid the whole story. Somehow, Tom felt he'd see the blond kid again. He was even more certain he would see Mabley again and, probably, Tony Costello. He wished he hadn't run into Mabley. He knew he wouldn't have, if he'd still had his job with Bernie. He'd be working somewhere, tearing down another old building, and wouldn't have the time to be bumming around like he was.

It made Tom all the more determined to find work again, for himself and for Jimmy. He stood with his friend and watched as Mabley and the cowboy walked over to the parking lot and got into a shiny new silver Audi. The drug racket was still paying well; Tom almost had to laugh to himself.

Mabley backed the car up, then waved to Tom before

driving out of the lot and pulling into traffic on Belmont Avenue.

"Let's go," Tom said, putting an arm around Jimmy's shoulder. "Steak and eggs? Maybe some wine?"

Jimmy loved it. "Medium rare and over-easy. Cabernet Sauvignon, 1972?"

When they got to the parking lot, Jimmy got in on the passenger side while Tom lowered himself into the driver's seat, aiming his key for the ignition switch.

Just as he sat down, Tom felt a sudden, strange sensation. The driver's seat crashed through the floor of the car and Tom felt himself falling hard and fast.

3

Suddenly, he stopped falling. Tom grabbed the steering wheel, dropped his keys, and looked in surprise at Jimmy seated next to him.

"What the hell?" Tom asked, then got out of the car and looked to see what had happened.

He knew the car was rusting apart. Paul had warned him about that and showed him the rust behind the driver's seat. Tom just hadn't expected the rust to spread so quickly and eat up the rest of the floor.

"The floor under the driver's seat is all gone," Tom told Jimmy as he came over to see for himself. "I didn't know because of the rubber mat covering the big hole. Look! The seat's not attached to anything anymore. No wonder it gave way! Lucky we weren't driving in traffic—I could have gone right through the floor and onto the street and lost control of the car."

Jimmy couldn't help himself. It was funny and he started laughing.

"If you could have seen your face, when you started to fall

through the floor!'' Jimmy said, nearly doubling up as he stood beside Tom.

It *was* funny, Tom had to admit, now that the initial shock had worn off. He began laughing, too.

"How the hell am I going to drive this heap home?" Tom asked. "I'm afraid to drive it ten feet, much less a dozen blocks."

He checked the problem out more closely, then managed to wedge the seat in so it didn't fall or move about so much. Sitting in the seat again, though gingerly, Tom found that if he didn't move or hardly breathed, the seat didn't fall or move too much. He'd chance it. He'd drive slowly and go down side streets. He wouldn't risk taking the car onto main streets with heavy midday traffic, in case the car took a sudden jolt. The seat really would fall through the floor the next time.

They didn't laugh, driving back to the warehouse. They both held their breath.

Halfway home, turning a corner, Tom felt the seat tilt to the right, then fall about an inch. He was already sitting farther back from the gas pedal and brake than he'd like, and about five inches lower than the seat should be. Luckily, the seat again wedged itself into place. Five minutes later, Tom pulled the old car into the alley behind the warehouse. He'd made it. Now he'd have to figure out how to put a new floor in the car, before driving it again.

All the way home, Tom remembered Earl Mabley's shiny new Audi. Wouldn't he love to be able to buy a new car like that! He could, if he went to work for Mabley and Costello, delivering drugs, like he figured the blond guy was doing. He'd never be able to afford a car like an Audi even if he got his old job back again. But the thought didn't stay in Tom's mind long. He knew that throwing in with Mabley and Costello was about the last thing he'd ever do. He'd fix up the

THE FINAL ACT

old VW so it would be safe to drive again, then he'd go out and look for work again, harder than before. He just wished he hadn't run into Mabley. He had enough to worry about without Mabley and Costello being back on the street.

Repairing the floor of the car occupied Tom and Jimmy for most of the next two days. Afterward, they pounded the pavement some more, looking for work.

"Nothing," Tom told Jimmy dejectedly as they stood on the corner of Broadway and Belmont after checking out a restaurant there. Tom had hoped one of them might get work waiting tables or even in the kitchen, but they both struck out. They had already asked Luigi Carmen for work at The Hot Spot but he couldn't put on any extra help. "I hate to say it, Jim-boy, but I'm about to give up."

Jimmy was trying to talk him out of giving up hope when a silver Audi pulled up to the restaurant.

"Buy you guys lunch?" a familar face asked them.

Tom recognized the driver. It wasn't Mabley or Costello, but the blond kid he'd seen with Mabley about a week before. He was still dressed like a rodeo rider, this time in a blue satin cowboy shirt and jeans.

"Thanks, we've got to be someplace," Tom said and motioned for Jimmy that they ought to take off.

"Sorry," the boy said, and Tom thought he meant it. "Maybe some other time? I don't really know anybody in town. I'm new here, from Colorado."

Go back there, Tom thought, walking off with Jimmy. Yet, in the back of his mind, Tom thought he might have been too hard on the guy. Maybe he'd just been suckered into working for Mabley, like he figured other kids were. They were out of work and needed money, and kids new to Chicago like the blond guy were especially easy targets for goons like Mabley and Costello. But he didn't want any part of them or whoever might be working for them now. As far as

Tom was concerned, what had happened with Mabley and Costello and the Guardians was all over now. He just wished the drug traffickers weren't thinking of maybe evening up the score.

"Yeah, we'll see you," Tom said casually over his shoulder as he went to his car.

He and Jimmy watched as the cowboy walked dejectedly toward the restaurant and then went inside.

"We didn't give him much of a chance," Jimmy said as he got into the passenger seat of the Volkswagen, beside Tom.

"I don't know," Tom said distractedly. "I think it's because he sort of reminds me of my old friend, Larry. The one I told you about, who got himself blown to pieces in a drug mix-up."

"Maybe we could give him some advice," Jimmy suggested.

But Tom put the key into the ignition and started the engine. "We probably could, but would he take it? He's new in town and needs money. He's getting it, but who knows at what price. We've got our own worries for now, anyway. What we need is something to *do*. Sometimes I think I need that even more than some money for doing it!"

They bummed around the rest of the afternoon and then got some spaghetti and ground beef and went up to the loft to make dinner for themselves and the other guys. It was Friday night and afterward, Tom and Maury went to their semimonthly probation Outreach volleyball game at a church gym on the far North Side. Paul Maggiore and some of the other probation officers got their guys together there to play some volleyball and rap a little. Jimmy took Ellie to a movie instead of joining them as he usually did. Marty had a babysitting job she couldn't miss. After Tom's mother died, Marty and Ellie kept the apartment they had shared, and the babysitting, plus another roommate, helped pay the rent.

THE FINAL ACT

After the game, Paul sat awhile with Tom and they talked about finding some work for him.

"I've asked everyone," Paul said dejectedly. "Even Mitchell Kowalski. I thought he'd have a job for you or know someone who might, but no luck. Times are really tough."

"Tell me about it," Tom said. He had too much nervous energy inside him to sit on the bench beside Paul, and he got to his feet and began shadow-boxing. "I'm spending most of my time in the gym. Maybe I could make a few bucks fighting."

"That would ruin your amateur standing," Paul reminded him.

Tom knew it, and knew he wouldn't take money to fight because he didn't want to mess up his Golden Gloves or Olympics chances somewhere down the line. But how else could he earn some money and keep himself busy? With nothing to do, he was going bananas.

"If you want to keep busy, why don't you do some volunteer work?" Paul suggested.

"You mean like at a hospital, changing bed pans, or driving lunches to old folk shut-ins?" Tom didn't think he was cut out for such things.

"How about suicide prevention?"

Tom looked at Paul and saw he was serious.

"What do I know about suicide prevention? Don't you have to be a shrink or something to handle heavy stuff like that?"

"Not necessarily," Paul explained. "I know a darned good volunteer agency called HelpLine. They're what's called a 'befriending' agency. They don't pretend to advise or counsel people who are close to taking their own lives. They're listeners. Lots of times, suicidal people just need someone willing to listen to what's troubling them. You don't even have to try and talk anyone out of killing themself. You just let them know you care enough about them to listen to their troubles."

Tom kept dancing around in front of Paul while his probation officer sat on the bench. He punched the air nervously; the green nylon jogging shorts in which he played volleyball were soaking wet from perspiration, and more sweat was beading up on his hairless bare chest.

"I don't know." Tom sighed, sitting back on the bench and dropping his arms between his legs. "It sounds like a downer. I'm down enough myself."

"Then you'd be a sympathetic listener," Paul said, putting a hand on Tom's knee. "Why don't you just try it, for an hour or two, maybe tomorrow? I'll give you the number to call."

"They'll think *I* need help," Tom quipped.

Paul got up and smiled. "Well, don't you? And, how about Jimmy, too? Maybe you'd go for it more, if he were into it, too. Keep you both off the streets for a while, until maybe I can find some paying work for you both."

Tom said he'd try it. It didn't thrill him, the thought of talking to people who were so low they were thinking of killing themselves. He didn't think he'd ever gotten that low himself, although at times he'd gotten pretty discouraged or overwhelmed.

"I think you'd make a good listener," Paul said, and they shook on it. He went to his locker and got out a pen and piece of paper and wrote a name and phone number on it and handed it to Tom. "Ask for Joe Grogan. He's the assistant director at the place and screens volunteers. I've already talked you up to him. And Jimmy, too."

Tom shrugged. "They're particular about whom they get to work for them for nothing."

Paul shook his head and laughed. "Why shouldn't they be

particular? Last month they saved about two hundred lives. Maybe one good listener saved one life. But it was a *good* listener."

Tom figured Grogan or somebody was probably going to train him and Jimmy on how to be good listeners. He never expected he'd be volunteering for anything, much less put up with being trained to work for nothing. But he *was* going bananas just hanging around street corners and hearing employment people tell him they weren't hiring. He'd try anything, even this.

4

Maury wanted to catch a late movie but Tom said he wanted to see Marty that night. He dropped Maury off at the loft and Maury, Scotty, Midget, and Wyllis went to the Biograph for a double feature of oldies—two Clark Gable and Spencer Tracy adventure movies, *Test Pilot* and *San Francisco*. They were two of Tom's and Paul's favorites, but Paul had a case he was on that night and Tom decided he'd rather see Marty.

Tom drove over to the apartment building half a dozen blocks from their own place and found Marty babysitting with a three-year-old girl and two-year-old boy. They were asleep in a playpen in the living room of the small apartment, and Marty had the TV on, watching a "Tonight Show" rerun with Joan Rivers guest-hosting. She was interviewing Christopher Reeve about *Superman III*.

Tom didn't like going to the apartment. It reminded him of his mother. She was only dead about a month and it had happened so fast and unexpectedly, getting hit by a car that Bernie's kid brother Steve had been driving, trying to shake off another car behind him with punk rockers spraying paint at him. His mother's dying words were for Tom to forgive Steve. It wasn't any use making trouble for him or trying to get even with him, Tom decided. It wouldn't bring his mother back.

He heard from Bernie that Steve seemed to be shaping up. He got off with probation for wreckless homicide and driving under the influence, considering another car was chasing his. The punk rock gang got busted up, and that was that. Steve was going to an alcohol treatment clinic and so was Marty's sister, Julie, who had started to drink heavily when Steve kept coaxing her to join him. It managed to turn Julie off to Steve and she was now going with a good guy, a young hospital orderly named Mark Hawley. Sometimes, Tom and Marty and Jimmy and Ellie triple-dated with Julie and Mark. Julie was back living at home with her folks and apparently things were finally going okay there. Julie's father no longer tried to get her into his bed, as he had tried with Marty. It had driven Marty to drugs and Julie to drink, but now both were off their poisons, and things seemed to be going okay again for them both. Steve he would just not worry about; he would have to find his own way. Tom might not hate him, to go along with his mother's dying wish, but he didn't see how he could ever like the kid.

A pretty, thin-looking girl came out of one of the bedrooms just as Marty let Tom into the apartment. He hadn't seen her before but Marty and his sister had told them a little about their new roommate. He wasn't quite prepared for how pretty she was or how skinny. *If she put some meat on her bones, she could be a real good-looker*, he thought. He liked her long, cornsilk blond hair and her angelic-looking face. She was a tiny thing; she looked like she was made of china.

Marty introduced Karen McCauley. She had a look of class about her that Tom liked. *She came from money*, he

THE FINAL ACT 33

thought. But then what was she doing on her own, at such a young age rooming with two other girls to save on rent? He didn't think she was even seventeen yet.

They shook hands and Karen's touch was so gentle Tom felt as though he had just shaken hands with a butterfly. She was so small and tiny and thin he thought he could blow her off her feet, if he took a deep breath. She wore a sleeveless blue blouse and white shorts. *It made her look even skinnier,* Tom thought. Like she had spent the winter at Buchenwald. But, God, she was still so pretty.

Karen curled up in an armchair and brushed her hair while glancing at a copy of *Seventeen*. Tom wished she'd leave him and Marty alone, but he figured the girl didn't want to be alone. Then he'd ignore her, Tom decided, making himself comfortable on the couch and snuggling up close to Marty.

He liked the perfume Marty had on, which smelled of spring flowers. He liked her long auburn hair and her very pretty face with the small straight nose, and he liked her deep brown eyes and her unpainted lips. She never wore makeup and he liked that—it was one of the best things about her. He hated girls who painted themselves up so you couldn't tell what they really looked like underneath. And she didn't wear just jeans, like most girls. She wore them that night, but often on their dates she'd wear a nice dress or skirt. He liked seeing her shapely legs and seeing her look feminine. Before Marty, dating some other girls had made Tom feel like he was dating another guy; they wore jeans and men's shirts and bomber jackets so they looked very masculine.

The kids in the playpen were asleep, so Marty didn't object to Tom holding her nor to a couple of well-placed kisses. When he seemed to want more, she pushed away his hands and gave him a look that reminded him she didn't want them to go at it hot and heavy. She liked him very much and once in a while even admitted she loved him, but she didn't want them to get too serious. They both had too much to do and too much growing up yet before they could even think of marrying. Tom grudgingly had to admit she was right, though lots of times he wished she wouldn't talk so sensibly. Maybe that was one of the main things he liked about her, that she had a head on her shoulders.

Marty had dreams of her own that included trying for the Olympics gymnastics team and applying for college and becoming a physical education instructor, like her mentor at her high school, Mrs. Sheridan. Mrs. Sheridan might have become an Olympic champion but she chose marriage over college, then when that went sour she finally went to night school and got her degree. She decided to devote her life to finding a girl to train for the Olympics so she could win the gold medal Mrs. Sheridan had not given herself the chance to win. Marty Marion was the girl she'd picked to win her dream for her, and, Tom sometimes realized jealously, her influence over Marty was often stronger than his own. But he began to make up his mind that that would be okay. Mrs. Sheridan was probably right. It would be better for Marty if she kept her focus on her dream, went to college, had her shot at the Olympics, then was qualified to teach gymnastics. If it was meant to be that he and Marty would someday get married, as he hoped it was, it would happen in its own right time.

If only he could be patient. That was one of the hardest things for Tom and he did his best to handle it. He couldn't even hope that maybe in a year or two, he and Marty could get a place of their own together. Marty denied she was especially religious, but she insisted she hadn't gone to bed with any guy yet and was saving herself for her husband on their wedding night. It sounded old-fashioned and sometimes even masochistic to Tom, to deny herself one of life's greatest pleasures. He ached for it most of the time he was with her, but he'd respect her feelings and judgment. Whatever she wanted of him was all right with him. He would even deny himself for her, knowing that was the way she wanted it. Thinking all that, he contented himself that night with pecking at her cheek.

Every so often, Tom saw Karen look at them and glance quickly back at her magazine if their eyes met. He wondered about her. She sure was pretty, though very young-looking. Like a young Grace Kelly, he decided. She was some father's and mother's little blond princess, maybe a long way from home. Who knows what sent her to live on her own. He could guess a hundred reasons, all of them very sad stories maybe involving divorce or child abuse or drugs or drinking or whatever. Maybe Karen had a father like Marty's and Julie's, who preferred his daughter to his wife. It was sick and Tom hated to think of things like that, yet knew it went on. He knew how it had nearly wrecked Marty's and Julie's lives, and he was glad he had been around to help both of them. Karen had some problem, he was sure of it; he knew the symptoms. Karen looked like a loner, a quiet girl who kept her problem or trouble to herself and found her own way to make it. He just met her and already he felt vaguely sorry for her. She was just too pretty to look so lonely and all-to-herself. She ought to be out that Friday night at some country club dance, the belle of the ball, being asked to dance by the most eligible sons of the richest families in Chicago. She was definitely a long way from home.

Tom didn't think that with Karen there it would be a good time to bring up the news that he was going to become a volunteer for a suicide prevention center. He nearly laughed, thinking how inappropriate that would be just then. He thought Karen might be able to use the phone number in his pocket, if she didn't cheer up soon.

An idea came to Tom. Maybe it was seeing how skinny

Karen was, but he suddenly had hunger pangs.

"I'll pop some corn," he suggested, getting up. "You got the kernels and oil?"

Marty left the couch and followed him into the kitchen. "Does a dog have fleas?" she quipped. "Does an elephant ever forget?"

She knew Tom's passion for popcorn. He rarely went without his nightly bowl. She always kept a bag of popping corn and a bottle of oil ready for his visits.

After popping a big bowl full of corn and salting it more than Marty liked, he carried it into the living room and offered some to Karen, but she declined.

"I'm on a strict diet," she said. Her voice was as soft as a breeze, too, and she went back to looking through her magazine.

A diet! Tom thought. She ought to be eating everything but the rug. Why was a skinny kid like her on a diet? If she lost any more weight, she wouldn't even cast a shadow!

Women, Tom figured, taking the popcorn bowl with him to the couch and slouching down to enjoy the rest of the "Tonight Show" and his girl beside him. He'd never figure them out if he lived to be as old as the guest who had just come on; he loved George Burns.

Tom had his arm around Marty and they were laughing at something George Burns said when suddenly Karen began to cry. She got up from her chair and ran to her room.

"What's with her?" Tom asked, surprised.

"We're not sure," Marty replied. "She doesn't do it often, but usually at the oddest times."

"She's so skinny. Does she eat at all?"

"She's out a lot. Ellie and I don't see her enough to know what she eats or if she eats regularly."

"Does she have enough money to buy food?" he asked.

Marty got up to check on the kids in the playpen. The

youngest had awakened and was crawling around. "She's paid her share of the rent and utilities so far, but she only joined us about a week ago. She didn't want to pool eating expenses, said she's into macrobiotic food—a lot of grains, mostly—and she eats at health food stores." She spoke softly so Karen wouldn't overhear.

"Does she go to school? How'd you meet her?"

"She dropped out last month," Marty said. "She's a junior, about sixteen. She answered a notice we put up on the bulletin board at the supermarket. We think she's a runaway, but she hasn't told us about herself. She just seemed kind of lost and lonely and scared. We figured we'd take her in and see how things went. Maybe we can find out what her problem is and help her."

She sympathized with the girl for being a runaway, and Tom knew why. Marty had been through it herself, when she ran away from her father.

"Well, let me know if I can help," Tom said just as the downstairs buzzer rang in the hallway.

The children's parents came to take them home and Tom hoped Marty would let him stay after they'd left. But she said she wanted to see how Karen was and, if the girl wanted, they could sit up awhile and talk.

Tom left the building and began driving home. On the way, he saw Jimmy walking down Belmont Avenue. He pulled over and stopped and gave his friend a lift.

Just as Tom drove onto the block where they lived he saw a silver car pull away from the curb and pass under a street lamp, then drive off. He couldn't make out who was at the wheel but thought the driver was alone. *Was it Mabley or Costello?* he wondered. Or maybe it was the blond guy from Colorado.

He was anxious about seeing the Audi near the warehouse until he and Jimmy got upstairs and found the rest of the

Guardians sitting up watching a late movie on TV. He decided to tell them about seeing the car and alert them that maybe they were in for some trouble from Mabley and Costello.

It was a real bummer, Tom thought. Things had been going reasonably well for a while. Now, he wasn't sure. He felt as if someone had dropped a shoe and he was waiting for the other to hit the floor.

5

Next morning, Tom didn't know what to do with the day. Marty said she needed the time to practice for a gym meet on Sunday and didn't want to go out that night.

After breakfast, it began to rain. It had rained more this April than it had been clear. It was beginning to get on Tom's nerves. He didn't like rainy or cloudy days; his spirits usually fell with the barometric pressure. Paul had told him that happens with most people, but some are more sensitive to the weather than others. Good sunshiny days make them feel great, but overcast or rainy days pull their spirits down.

He wasn't eager to check out the phone number of the suicide prevention center Paul had given him the night before, figuring he felt down enough. But the overriding feeling of desperation to do something besides work out at the gym made Tom suggest to Jimmy that they look into the possibility of volunteering at the center. Jimmy agreed; they could at least check it out.

Tom made the call and got to talk to Joe Grogan. He told them a little about the program over the phone but suggested they come over if they were interested in volunteering. Tom decided that if he was going to do it, he'd do it right then and drove over to the center with Jimmy.

They found the place on Sheridan Road up near Montrose, not far north of the warehouse. It was HelpLine's North Side office but they had two others, west and south. This one was in a former neighborhood department store, a vanished breed of neighborhood life that had passed with the advent of the shopping center and discount store. Two big windows overlooked the street. Inside were rows of old desks where six or eight people sat, answering telephones or doing some kind of paperwork. They were of all ages; Tom saw some senior citizens, middle-aged men and women, and a couple of teenagers.

No phones were ringing when they entered the center late that morning. An old woman at one phone was talking softly and they couldn't hear what she was saying. A teenage girl directed them to the back of the place where a man Tom figured to be in his mid-thirties sat at a desk. He stood up when Tom and Jimmy approached him.

Joe Grogan, tall, good-looking, with thick brown hair and mustache and intense brown eyes, introduced himself. He shook their hands enthusiastically and Tom liked him immediately. After they sat down, Grogan gave them a short spiel on why the center was there and what the volunteers did. It was just as Paul had told Tom. The center was not a referral service to give out psychiatrists' names, or even for advising or counseling.

"We're listeners," Grogan explained. He looked businesslike, in a lightweight tan suit, blue shirt, and yellow and blue striped tie. "We're what we call a 'befriending' agency. We have about fifty trained volunteers and get about two hundred phone calls a month from people who are lonely and depressed. The number increases a hundred percent or more each month. That shows there's a real need for a service like this."

Services like HelpLine got started over the last thirty years, Grogan told them, and this one was established at that time but had operated under various names earlier. They were patterned after an organization that began in the early 1950s in England.

"A fourteen-year-old English girl killed herself when she thought her first menstrual period was a sign that she had venereal disease," Grogan said. "The minister who conducted the funeral service for the girl thought something ought to be done to keep tragedies like that from happening to others. He started holding tea meetings to talk about sexual matters but soon found that people who came had many other problems and hang-ups. They came because they found the minister was a sympathetic listener. Before long, the tea sessions led to him starting a suicide prevention center. The idea crossed the Atlantic soon after and centers began cropping up in this country.

"Statistics show we're providing a good service. And our own records here show that not one of the people who've called us threatening suicide has gone ahead and killed himself. They were either talked out of it or were given medical treatment in time. We alert police or paramedics if someone who has actually done something to take their own life calls."

It's pretty strong stuff, Tom thought. He liked what he heard and saw while he sat listening with Jimmy. Jimmy looked at him and nodded that he went for it, too.

"We don't know anything about how to handle it, if someone called and we had to try and talk them out of killing themselves," Tom admitted.

"None of us here did, either, before we got some training," Grogan replied. "We have training sessions for volunteers to learn how to sympathize with callers, and how to lead the conversation into the reasons why the caller is thinking of committing suicide.

"You listen for a hint to the problem that's making the caller feel depressed or overwhelmed or uptight. In other sessions you learn about the causes of suicidal feelings such as depression, grief, sexual problems, alcoholism, drug abuse."

Tom had firsthand experience at most of those things. He thought he might catch on fast at the training sessions.

"The main thing is," Grogan confided, "you make sure the caller knows that whatever he tells you is strictly confidential. And it's the caller's time. He can do whatever he wants on his twenty cents. He can yell, scream, cry, do or say whatever he wants. Your job is to listen and sympathize and try to talk him out of taking his life."

Tom began to relax and grow more involved, pulled in by the enthusiasm and dedication of the young man. In some ways, Grogan reminded him of Paul Maggiore. He didn't bring Paul up, but he figured they knew each other and were probably friends. He wasn't asked about his own background and neither was Jimmy. Grogan gave the impression that he wasn't interested in prying. Tom and Jimmy were just two guys who came in off the street and wanted to help. Grogan would accept them from there, Tom felt, and he especially liked that arrangement.

As Grogan explained more about the center and suicide prevention, they learned more about the main reasons many people called HelpLine.

"We're hearing more and more from teenagers who don't seem to have any sense of their own lives anymore," he said. "Kids call us because they find it easier to talk to a stranger over the phone than face a counselor. They spill their guts to us because we're sympathetic and don't make judgments.

"Lots of people are out of work and depressed—everyone from teenagers to senior citizens. They're not only uptight about not having money to pay the bills and to live on, but they don't know what to do with their time. They're literally climbing the walls."

Tom knew how that was. That was why he'd come there.

"While we're listening, we try to find something in the caller's life that he finds worthwhile," Grogan continued. "We might ask when the last time was that he felt good about himself. Often that can help snap a person out of feeling a sense of hopelessness.

"If the caller still sounds bent on suicide, we try to talk him into putting it off at least a day; maybe tomorrow things will look better, or by then he can get some help. We work with some people hour-by-hour. If we can talk someone into living day-by-day, it's good. It can lead to the caller finding a way out besides taking his own life, committing the final act."

With that background, Grogan explained more about the training sessions—six three-hour sessions they could start in on right away that afternoon. Afterward, they could set up a volunteering schedule. Volunteers manned the phones twenty-four hours a day, every day of the week. They worked in shifts around the clock, agreeing to serve at least four hours a week for six months.

Tom and Jimmy agreed they wanted to go for it. Grogan got up again, shook their hands once more, and walked them over to an older woman who took it from there. She arranged for them to join the next training session after lunch.

It was still raining when they left the center. Tom looked at Jimmy and shook his head. "I need to burn off some nervous energy," he said. "How about we go to the gym and work out a little, then catch some lunch and be back here for the first training session?"

Jimmy agreed and they drove over to Turner Park and changed into boxing trunks, shoes, and gloves. Though Jimmy couldn't take chances in a real boxing match anymore, he could spar with Tom—they did that for almost an hour. Tom was always careful not to hit Jimmy on the head or to make him fall.

Tom began to feel better. He'd liked Joe Grogan and felt like he wanted to become a volunteer at the suicide prevention center. But he knew it wasn't going to be easy, especially since he was uptight himself about being unemployed. He'd already heard and seen a lot of sad stories in his young life, and he expected to become involved in a lot more in the weeks ahead. Sparring with Jimmy while thinking about it all made him forget for a moment and he nearly landed a mean right to Jimmy's head. Jimmy saw it coming and ducked just in time. He laughed but Tom got shook up by it and stopped and hugged his friend. He promised he'd keep his concentration in the future. It was what Johnny Lynch had kept telling him, that concentration was half the battle.

It gave Tom an idea as they continued sparring. He'd concentrate on the volunteer training sessions. Maybe it could help him push everything else out of his mind. He'd live day-to-day himself, until he would land a new job or get back on Bernie's construction crew.

Tom knew he was lucky. He had someone to talk to about things when he needed or wanted to. He had Jimmy and the other guys and his sister and Marty, too. Communication, he remembered. It had been what he was after for so long, wishing people would open up to each other and talk things out when times got tough. Most of the time, even without any other help, just talking things out with somebody willing to listen was enough. After that, things usually sorted themselves out and problems got worked out. It was possible then to live hour-by-hour, then day-by-day. That was about all

THE FINAL ACT

any of them could expect, to be able to live day-by-day.

Jimmy threw a good left that caught Tom on the chin by surprise. Tom stumbled back and landed on the canvas on the seat of his white trunks so he bounced twice. Sitting on the floor with his legs wide apart, a stunned look on his face, he realized that his friend had put the punch there to teach him the lesson of concentration all over again.

6

That afternoon, Tom and Jimmy got in on an introductory session at the center and heard some more horror stories about suicide, especially among teenagers. Joe Grogan conducted the training session. Suicide, he said, was now the main cause of death among those between the ages of fifteen and twenty-four, taking the dubious title away from senior citizens, who formerly held it.

One of the true stories that got to Tom was about the eighteen-year-old girl who was afraid of going away to college and not doing well enough, and who hanged herself the first night she got there.

"Many young people today aren't ready for the process of success or failure," Grogan told the small group of volunteers in a back room at the center. "They think success has to be instantaneous. And maybe their parents try to mold them as an extension of themselves. They want to live their lives over again through their kid by making the kid go the route the parents, for one reason or another, didn't get to go. The parent missed some opportunity or didn't have the money or the guts or whatever to pursue his goal in life, like the type of work he wanted to do. So the kid is supposed to do the thing the parent never did. The kid doesn't have a chance to have a life of his own."

Tom thought of Mrs. Sheridan, Marty's gymnastics coach. The shoe fit her perfectly. She hadn't been able to enter the Olympics because she got married too early, so later she began pushing Marty to be the Olympic gold medal winner the coach hadn't been. The pressure nearly cost Marty her life, when she'd turned to look-alike drugs.

"Kids don't want to tell their parents about their problems or what's worrying them," Grogan said. "They don't want to let their parents down, or they simply can't or won't communicate with them.

"There's a bond of silence between teenagers today that is bad and dangerous. If a teenager tells a friend he's going to commit suicide and asks the friend to keep it to himself, the friend expects to have to keep that pledge of silence. Often, the friend doesn't take such a threat seriously. But it should be taken seriously and they should tell someone about it so the kid can be helped."

After that, Grogan introduced the older woman in the center, and she began telling them how to handle the phone calls and develop ways of becoming a good listener.

Though he had expected the time to drag, Tom thought the two hours went by like ten minutes. He found himself tuning in a lot more than he thought he would. Jimmy did, too, asking even twice as many questions as Tom.

They hung around the center for another half hour after the first training session, to watch and hear some of the other volunteers at work. None of it was what Tom could consider enjoyable work, except in the way that they felt they were doing something meaningful to help other people who really needed someone to talk to. The sense of being needed re-

THE FINAL ACT 49

minded Tom of how he felt about the Guardians. They stuck together because they needed each other, and Tom felt good about having organized the guys because it gave him a sense of being needed.

Later, driving back to the warehouse, Jimmy spotted the silver Audi. The blond guy, in cowboy clothes again, was coming out of an apartment building and got into the car. They saw Mabley behind the wheel and Costello in the back seat with some girl, but they didn't get a good look at her because Mabley drove away from the curb and into traffic. She looked very young, Jimmy told Tom, but neither of them thought they recognized her.

"They're recruiting girls now, too, I suppose," Tom said. "I admit, I expected trouble from Mabley and Costello, but so far they haven't tried anything."

"Let's follow them," Jimmy suggested. "Maybe the two kids they've got with them will get out of the car later and we'll have a chance to talk to them. We could warn them about who they're getting mixed up with."

Tom went for the idea and began maneuvering the car into the traffic on Broadway until he got only a few car lengths behind the Audi. After about another half-dozen blocks, Mabley turned the car up Addison Street and headed toward Wrigley Field, then pulled over in front of an apartment building on Fremont, only about two blocks from Cubs' Park. The blond guy got out, stuffing something in his pants pocket. Tom couldn't tell if it was money or drugs as he parked far enough away so they wouldn't be seen.

"Maybe he lives there or is just delivering some stuff," Tom thought aloud.

"Whichever, we know where this place is," Jimmy said as they saw the Audi start to drive away. "Let's follow to see where the girl goes."

Tom liked Jimmy's thinking and waited until the Audi was

safely ahead of them before beginning to follow. As they passed the building the blond boy had entered, Jimmy saw him check the mailboxes and stand in the hallway looking at some mail.

"He must live there," Jimmy surmised, "or why would he be checking mail there? If he was making a delivery, he'd go right to an apartment."

It made sense to Tom. "We can go back and talk to him later."

They followed the Audi for about half a mile into rush-hour traffic but got stuck behind a van at a stoplight and lost sight of the car.

It was raining hard again and Tom's wipers began acting up, so they could hardly see through the windshield. He decided against going back to check on the blond boy just then, since they were so close to home, and they drove home instead.

They were running low on food money. Tom stopped first at a supermarket and checked out the meat sales. He told Jimmy they'd had so much chicken lately, because it was cheap, he was almost starting to lay eggs. Liver was cheap, but he didn't know how to fix it. He got tired of waiting to find a butcher to ask, so he bought the beef liver, some frozen french fries, and three cans of mixed vegetables. Tom had learned a trick or two about cooking, and Jimmy had a few dishes he knew how to make. Together they took over the dinner chores.

The other guys were home watching the tube when they got there. They had a phone message for Tom and Jimmy. Joe Grogan needed two extra volunteers for that night, midnight to four A.M., if they could make it. He knew they weren't fully trained yet, but they could use them for that emergency and they could speed up the training in the next few days.

THE FINAL ACT

Tom called the center and said they would both be there at midnight.

"Liver's like pork, isn't it?" Tom asked Jimmy as they started to prepare dinner.

"Yeah, I think it's got to fry a long time or you get worms or something," Jimmy replied. "I think you flour it and then put salt and pepper on top and fry the hell out of it for half an hour or something."

It sounded reasonable to Tom. They would fry the liver until any chance of getting trichinosis would be burned out of the meat. They laughed, remembering the time Jimmy had mistaken powdered sugar for flour and fried them up some candied pork chops.

Tom stood over the frying pan and watched as the floured liver began to sizzle and the oil in the pan began to turn brown and start smoking. He added more oil and kept turning the slices of liver for nearly half an hour, until the smoke got so thick in the kitchen that it set off their ceiling smoke alarm and Jimmy opened all the windows, letting in the rain.

Jimmy took the french fries out of the oven and Tom brought the frying pan to the table as the other guys sat and wondered about the charred-looking shreds of meat Tom began to put on their plates.

"Catsup goes good with liver, I think," Tom said, setting a bottle of catsup on the table, then sitting to cut into his own slice of meat.

"Tough, ain't it?" Jimmy observed, unable to cut through his piece of liver. He gave Tom a sly smile.

"Not mine," Tom insisted, having a hard time slicing a piece off his liver. Finally, he gave up and took the piece in his fingers and began trying to chew it.

Maury tried chewing his liver, too, then gave up. "We could use these as hockey pucks, if it was winter."

Tom took his plate to the window, reached out, and they all listened as the slice of charred liver fell from his plate and down from the second floor of the warehouse to the pavement below. They heard a little thud as the liver hit the concrete.

"Well, we can always go back to chicken," Jimmy joked; and they all went back to the table to make do with the fries and heated-up vegetables.

Wyllis and Scotty did the dishes and Maury and Midget watched a rerun of "M*A*S*H" while Tom and Jimmy drove over to see Marty and Ellie. When they got there, they were both glad to see that the girls' roommate, Karen, wasn't there. Marty said Karen had gone out to a health food restaurant and wasn't back yet.

They didn't stay long, because Marty reminded Tom she had to get her rest, to be up for the gym meet the next afternoon. The four of them sat on the couch and watched a made-for-tv potboiler about a hatchet maniac and Tom wondered why they were watching such garbage until he flicked the dial and tuned in *Young Frankenstein*, which suited them all better.

Tom seemed to need Marty more than he could ever remember before. He put his arm around her on the couch and they kissed, but when he began to make his moves, Marty resisted. She had to tell him again that she didn't want them to get so serious. She didn't belabor the point, not wanting to embarrass him in front of his sister and best friend. But he got her message. She implied that Jimmy and Ellie were able to go a little slower and that's how she hoped Tom could be with her.

He knew she was right, but it still frustrated him. He got up impatiently and Jimmy could see he was ready to leave. Jimmy said good night to Ellie with a final kiss and they left, an hour early for their volunteer work.

Tom thought they'd kill the hour before midnight by driving over to the apartment building where they thought the boy

THE FINAL ACT

who was working for Mabley and Costello lived. Just as Tom pulled the car onto Fremont near Cubs' Park, they saw the blond boy leaving the building. He got into a cab and it drove off to the north.

Tom followed, cursing his worn wiper blades as rain continued to wash out his vision. The cab drove eastward to the high rises along Sheridan Road overlooking Lincoln Park, then stopped. The guy got out and the cab waited while he ran into the lobby of a high rise.

Tom and Jimmy waited in the car, parked not far away. After only about ten minutes, the blond boy was back, running for the taxi again in the rain. The cab made an illegal U-turn on Sheridan and sped southward. Tom figured the guy had to make several deliveries that night by cab; there wasn't time to follow him on all his rounds. He headed for the suicide prevention center. They would still check out the blond guy later, and warn him to break with Mabley and Costello before it was too late. Guys who went to work for them either wound up in jail or the trunk of a car before finding a place in the morgue. He thought it would be too bad if the blond guy wound up that way. But it would be even worse, he began thinking, if the girl they'd seen with the drug pushers wound up like that.

Joe Grogan was there when they arrived about fifteen minutes early. Tom thought he looked tired, but he was talking to the other volunteers and checking on things and being as busy and involved as ever.

"Two of our regulars came down with colds or flu," Grogan explained to Tom and Jimmy when he saw them come in the center. "We were desperate for fill-ins."

He laughed when he realized what a put-down that sounded like.

"I just mean, you can get more training but we really need you tonight," he explained.

Tom said they understood and laughed it off. They sat with

an older black man who was manning one of the telephones. They could hear only what he was saying to someone who had called HelpLine, but they got the gist of it. A girl was on the line, crying, and saying she had to talk to someone about the bad time she was having with her boyfriend. It didn't sound as if she were threatening suicide, however. She just needed someone to talk to about it all. It was serious, though, Tom figured. At least to her.

The black man and a blond woman in her thirties were the only volunteers, besides Tom and Jimmy, who remained at midnight.

As Grogan was leaving, Tom assured him they'd be all right. Chances were, Grogan said, it would be a quiet night. They hadn't gotten many calls in the past few hours. The more experienced volunteers would take all the calls if they could handle them. Tom and Jimmy would take any overflow.

After two hours, Jimmy fell asleep at his desk and his phone never rang. Tom sat at a desk between Jimmy's and the black man's, listening as the man, Earl Spencer, took an occasional call.

"It *is* a quiet night," Spencer said to Tom, after taking a call from a senior citizen woman who complained her landlord wasn't sending up enough heat and she was chilled.

"Lots of people don't know what HelpLine is," the tall, thin man in jeans and a blue sweater told Tom. "They think we're like those newspaper or television consumer complaint services. It's okay. If we're not busy and can help them, we do. I didn't know what to tell the woman who just called, except to put on a sweater and bang on the radiator."

Rain kept coming down hard outside. Tom felt the strangeness of the early morning. It was half past two and he always considered himself a night person, enjoying staying out late. But this was different. He was in an officelike place

THE FINAL ACT 55

and outside of some soft music playing on a radio, the center was quiet as a church, except when a phone rang once in a while. He wasn't used to just sitting in a place like that in the early hours of the morning. If he was out that late, he'd be at some video game place or parked somewhere in his car with Marty.

Two calls came at once a little while later, and the woman and Spencer took them. While they were talking to their callers, at about three o'clock, another call came in. Tom got it before Jimmy and heard a girl on the line.

Tom had heard how Spencer answered his calls and followed his style.

"Hi, how're you doing?" Tom asked the girl.

She didn't answer for a while, but he knew she was there.

"Lousy," she finally replied. "Do you think I'd call if I felt great?"

He allowed her that. "My name's Tom. You don't have to tell me yours."

"I won't," she said sharply. "You sound young."

"So do you. I'm nearly eighteen. But I feel a lot older."

"You some kind of goddamn do-gooder?" she challenged.

He thought a moment. "I hope so. At least, I hope I can do someone some good, sometime."

She fell silent again for a while. Then she sighed and began talking with less hostility. "I guess I'm all fucked up, that's why I called. Someone I know gave me the number. She called here once, when she was thinking of . . . taking a lot of stuff."

The girl sounded younger than seventeen, Tom thought. She didn't sound as if she were on anything. She just sounded angry, frustrated, and very uptight.

Tom waited for her to get to why she had called, but she was in no hurry to tell him.

"I'm sixteen," she told him. "This guy really treated me lousy."

She fell silent again but Tom had seen how Spencer handled situations like that. "Maybe if you talked to me about it, you'd feel better."

Spencer finished with his call by then and sat listening to Tom. Tom motioned to him, as if to suggest that if Spencer thought it best, he could take the call from there. But Spencer nodded that he thought Tom was doing fine and should keep trying to draw the caller out.

It gave Tom a good feeling, a sense of confidence he hadn't felt before in wondering how he would handle his first caller. When the girl still hesitated about telling him more about the trouble she was having with some guy, he said the same thing again, only a little differently.

"It's your twenty cents," Tom suggested. "I'm not doing anything better. You don't know me, I don't know you. We probably never will. Why not let it all hang out? Who knows, maybe I can even cheer you up."

She laughed ruefully, then sounded as if she were beginning to relax. "Okay, what the heck. Tom, I'm about as low as I've ever been. You know what I mean? My folks go at it every night like Luke Skywalker and Darth Vader. My father's an alky, Mom's on something, I don't know what. They're loaded, you know what I mean? They've got money. I come from a real high-class family. Big house in Wilmette, you know?"

He could imagine. One of the big mansions along Lake Michigan on Chicago's exclusive North Shore. He figured rich people had most of the same problems as poor people in the inner city, except they probably didn't have money to worry about.

"I split, about three months ago," the girl went on. "I took some money with me and got a place by myself and then

THE FINAL ACT 57

I met this guy, Floyd. God, what a hunk! But a real airhead, you know what I mean? He's gorgeous, but nothing upstairs. Hell, I didn't care. We liked each other and he moved in with me and we had good times." She began to laugh. "Boy, did we have good times!"

Tom caught the edge of pain in her laugh. Apparently, the good times hadn't lasted long and obviously were now over.

"I thought we had something going," she said after a while. "Something good. But he didn't stay long. Off and on, I think it was only two weeks. He kept hanging around with some friends of his, guys and girls. There's a girl named Betty he likes. I think she's a bigger airhead than he is. But, anyway, he split two weeks ago and I'm going nuts. I'm not calling from where I live, so my roommates can't hear me. I tried keeping the place I had by myself, but I started climbing the walls. Without Floyd, it seemed like a dump and just nothing. I guess it's all over with Floyd. I saw him tonight. He was with Betty and it nearly blew my mind, you know what I mean?"

It was an old, sad story, Tom thought. But new and painful to the girl. How could he help her? he wondered. It made him wonder how he'd feel if, suddenly, Marty took up with some other guy.

"Oh, what the hell!" the girl said hopelessly. "I'm not gonna go off the deep end. At least, I don't think I am. I've got some stuff here that could do it, but I'm not thinking of doing it. At least, I don't think I am. I don't know. You know what I mean?"

He wasn't sure. He listened and waited, but she fell silent again. Then she began to sound all choked up and he couldn't understand what she was saying.

Finally, she got hold of herself and laughed nervously. "I'll be okay," she said.

"Sure you will," Tom encouraged her. "Turn on the tv.

Watch something to take your mind off things. Keep talking. I'm not doing anything. I'll listen as long as you want."

She rambled on after that. Sometimes she talked more about Floyd, sometimes she laid into Betty and Tom nearly stopped listening because he didn't really want to hear all that, but he hung on. Spencer looked sympathetic. He'd been through long calls like that before—calls that seemed to drift in many directions.

Finally, the girl said she felt better and she would hang up. Occasionally he heard noises in the background, from wherever she was calling. It was either a restaurant or someplace where she was using a public phone and people were not far away, or she was at somebody's apartment.

"Thanks, Don," she said, as if about to hang up.

He didn't bother correcting her about his name. She hadn't used it in ten minutes and had forgotten what it was.

"You don't sound like such a bad guy," she said, then sounded as if that was funny. "Considering you're a guy. You know what I mean?"

7

Tom didn't get to handle any more calls that morning. The few that came in later were handled by Spencer and the woman. Jimmy didn't get to handle any calls but felt he'd learned a lot. So did Tom. He didn't think being a volunteer there would be any easy thing. What he realized most from the girl's call was that a life hung in the balance on the other end of the line. Someone was so desperate they were ready to end their life, and maybe the phone call they were making, to reach out for help from a stranger, would be their last chance.

Two more volunteers came in at four in the morning to take over the phones. Spencer and the woman told Tom he'd done a good job and they all left.

A fine drizzle was coming down. It still looked dark as midnight outside and though Jimmy was sleepy, Tom felt strangely wide awake, too awake to go home to bed. He got Jimmy to agree to get some hot chocolate someplace; they both hated coffee.

The Volkswagen was parked on a nearby side street. Walking toward it, they thought they heard a car door close behind them on the street. Turning, they saw the Audi. Two big guys were running toward them. In the dark, Tom couldn't tell who they were but didn't think they were Mabley, Costello, or the blond guy their age.

They ran for the car but before they reached it, two more guys came out of nowhere ahead of them and they found themselves trapped. There was no street lamp near the car, and in the dark Tom couldn't make out any of the guys.

Tom and Jimmy looked at each other, realizing they were outnumbered. The four guys were older and bigger than they, but they would put up the best fight they could. Tom only worried that the guys would hurt Jimmy's head.

At first, they exchanged some blows with the four guys, but after only a few minutes, they were overpowered. After the attackers had Tom and Jimmy on the sidewalk beside their car, they began kicking them until they both lost consciousness.

Tom came to later, in a daze. Two cops were looking him and Jimmy over. Tom had no idea how long he'd been lying there, and he didn't know where he hurt the most. He seemed to hurt all over.

His first concern was for Jimmy. He half-crawled to where Jimmy lay facedown near the rear of the car. Jimmy was still unconscious, his face bloody and bruised.

"Get an ambulance for him," Tom pleaded to the officers. "He had a bad head injury a couple of months ago."

"What happened here?" one of the cops asked while his partner went back to their squad car to call for an ambulance.

"Four guys came after us," Tom explained, managing to get to one knee and feeling as if he'd just been knocked out after going ten rounds with the four guys.

"Why?" the cop asked. "Did you recognize any of them?"

"It was too dark," Tom said, getting shakily to his feet. "I

THE FINAL ACT

don't know why they were after us. Probably to rob us." He didn't want to involve the cops in his trouble with Mabley and Costello, at least not yet.

"Put your hands over your head," the cop told Tom impatiently, then raised Tom's arms for him. "You got anything on you?" he asked.

"Just a few dollars," Tom insisted. "No drugs, if that's what you mean. No weapon, either."

"We'll see," the cop said, then patted Tom down. "It don't make sense, four guys beating the two of you up like this, for just a couple of bucks."

Tom couldn't see what he looked like. The cop saw a boy with a bloody nose, an old cut over one eye that had opened up again, red bruises all over his face, and his yellow shirt bloody and torn. Tom was wearing his dead friend Larry's yellow silk sportshirt, or what was left of it.

Not finding any weapon or drugs on Tom, the cop wasn't satisfied with the routine pat-down. He moved behind Tom and began a thorough body search. Tom stood there impatient and angry, complaining that the cops ought not to be wasting their time checking him and Jimmy out. They ought to be out trying to catch the guys who beat them up.

While the cop kept searching Tom, the other one came back after calling for an ambulance and began going over Jimmy as he lay unconscious. A fine rain still came down on them.

Tom felt the cop's big hands moving over his pockets, probing inside them, then move over the front of his blue jeans, then up inside his belt line. They stopped there and then the cop drew something out.

"What's this?" the cop asked, holding up a long, white plastic package. Not opening it, he took a whiff. "Well what do you know. *La Dama Blanca*. Coke. It looks pure, too. I suppose you don't know how that got inside your pants."

Tom couldn't believe what was happening. "No," he said helplessly. "I don't."

But he knew how it got there. After beating up him and Jimmy, the musclemen had planted the cocaine on him. He hoped they hadn't done the same on his friend.

The cop went over Tom again even more thoroughly, while his partner searched Jimmy closer, even as the sound of an ambulance siren wailed toward them.

"Nothing on this one," the other cop reported after going over Jimmy.

Tom was relieved to hear that. Moments later, paramedics arrived and looked Jimmy over, then lifted him onto a stretcher and drove off with him to Grant Hospital.

Tom pleaded to be able to go with Jimmy, but the cop who had found the cocaine on him handcuffed Tom's hands behind him, then roughly began moving him toward the squad car.

"You're coming with us," the cop said. "To the station, to be strip-frisked."

Tom still couldn't believe any of this was happening to him. He didn't try to resist and gave up trying to convince the cops the coke had been a mistake. When he insisted it had been planted on him, they laughed. They'd heard that one before.

Tom's main worry wasn't that drugs had been found on him. Somehow, he felt he could clear that up. What worried him more was wondering how badly Jimmy had been hurt. Had the goons hit him on the head badly, or had Jimmy hit his head on the sidewalk when he fell? Tom wanted to be with his friend. He looked around desperately in the back seat of the squad car as he was being driven to the police station, but there was no escape. He felt helpless and desperate.

He also hurt all over and he began to feel groggy. The paramedics had checked him over quickly but thought he was

THE FINAL ACT

just shook up and not seriously hurt. Their main concern was to get Jimmy to the hospital as fast as they could, and the cops wouldn't let them take Tom along. They insisted they had to take Tom to the station and book him.

Tom hardly knew what was happening to him at the station. He was booked on possession of narcotics and, before he knew it, he was in an interrogation room.

"Take off your clothes," a burly black cop told Tom after he entered the room with the two arresting officers and a narcotics detective. The detective also was black and built like a linebacker.

"I already got searched half a dozen times," Tom insisted.

"A strip-frisk is routine in such cases," the detective advised Tom in a manner that suggested that Tom should be as cooperative as possible and maybe he'd receive fair treatment.

Tom reluctantly began to unbutton what was left of his shirt. His fingers hurt and he found they were clumsy and slow. The burly cop lost his patience with Tom. He stripped Tom down to his boxer shorts and, looking disappointed when no more narcotics were found on him, looked through his clothes.

The narcotics detective introduced himself as Alvin Ward. He had on a blue blazer and gray slacks, his striped tie loosened at the neck. He seemed okay to Tom, just a dick doing his job. Ward didn't seem as hostile to him as the three cops in the room.

The room was small, with a wash basin in one corner. The only window in the room had iron bars on it. Tom could tell it was raining harder outside. The room was too hot, and the air so dry Tom could hardly breathe.

"You can put your clothes back on now," Ward told Tom after the burly cop finished looking through Tom's jeans and dropped them and the shirt on the floor.

"Now what's this I hear you claim the coke was planted on you?" Ward asked Tom.

Tom had done some thinking and decided he'd better tell the truth, even if it meant bringing the cops down again on Mabley and Costello. He told Ward the whole story, including how he had been responsible for blowing the whistle on Mabley and Costello a few months earlier and breaking up their look-alike drug racket.

Ward looked at Tom suspiciously. "I thought they locked up Mabley and Costello. Every cop in Chicago knows about Costello. We're glad he got caught, he gave us all a bad name. But you're telling me he's out on the street again and up to his old tricks?"

When Tom insisted it was true and, seeing that Ward still looked skeptical, he suggested the detective call his probation officer. By the wall clock, Tom could tell it was not quite five in the morning, and he didn't want Paul awakened at such an hour, but he felt he had no choice. The detective and the cops looked like they were ready to lock him up and throw away the key.

"I've got one phone call coming, don't I?" Tom reminded Ward.

Grudgingly, the detective motioned for Tom to use the phone on the desk in the room. Tom dialed Paul Maggiore's home phone number, but there was no answer after he let it ring nearly a dozen times. Feeling helpless and for the first time a little scared, Tom put down the phone.

"Does that count?" he asked the detective. "I didn't get to talk to anybody."

"You're wasting your time with this one," the cop who had first searched Tom told the detective. "He's just trying to stall for time. Let's put him in the lock-up so we can get out of here."

THE FINAL ACT

Ward looked at the cop and Tom could tell the detective didn't care much for the uniformed officer.

"I'll take care of the kid," Ward told the other three officers. "I'll call if I need you."

The cops reluctantly left the room and Ward told Tom he could use the basin to wash up.

Tom got a drink of water he'd been wanting badly; the room was so hot and dry he felt like his tongue was made of cardboard. Then he looked in a mirror over the wash basin and saw that the old boxing cut over his left eye had reopened and that blood, together with blood from his nose, had made a real mess of his face. After wiping it off with some paper towels from a wall dispenser, he ran his hands through his thick black hair because his comb had been taken from him by the arresting officers, together with his wallet and other things he'd had on him.

He was starting to feel a little less groggy, though his neck began to hurt quite a bit. Mainly he began to worry again about Jimmy. Was he okay? What were they doing to him in the hospital?

"How about that phone call?" Tom asked Ward after he'd cleaned up a little. "I'd like to call my sister."

Ward told Tom it would be okay and Tom sat at the desk and dialed Ellie. She was frightened at being called so early in the morning, and he wished he hadn't had to do it, but he needed to talk to her, about himself and about Jimmy. She'd want to know how Jimmy was, about as much as he did.

She listened to him, then said she'd go right to the hospital or come to the police station, whichever Tom wanted.

"Go to Grant Hospital," Tom told her. "I'm okay here. I think Paul can straighten things out for me, but I've got to know how Jim-boy is. Let me know soon as you can. But keep trying to reach Paul for me, okay?"

She promised she would do as he asked, and she would contact the other guys back at the loft, too.

After making the call, Tom had to tell his story all over again to the detective. Tom's neck hurt more than ever and his head ached so he could hardly think. Above everything was his worry that Jimmy was badly hurt. At times he hardly heard Ward's questions, his mind was so preoccupied wondering about his friend.

Had Jimmy's old head injury come back? If he was really hurt bad, Tom knew what he would do. He would go after Mabley and Costello himself this time. He'd make sure neither of them got a chance to hurt his friend again. He'd fix them so they wouldn't get back out on the street again, no matter who they paid off.

There was so little left of the yellow silk shirt he had on, Tom felt half-undressed and, because of that, even more helpless and vulnerable. The shirt began to remind him of who it had first belonged to. He had loved Larry like a brother, but Larry started to fall apart from drinking and drugs until he got himself blown apart.

It was the sight of Larry lying dead in his own blood, so badly shot up that even Tom could hardly recognize his once handsome face, that had started to turn Tom around. Before that, Tom had been willing to keep following Larry, into whatever horror Larry led him, because he trusted Larry and there was no other direction he could see for himself.

So far, he felt he'd done pretty good, turning away from his old ways. He played it smart and cool for nearly a year, forming the Guardians, and responsibly handling the rough times that had followed. People had always been trying to sucker him and his friends into doing their dirty work for them, delivering drugs, using them any way they could. Tom had done what he could, then when he needed help he'd gone to Paul for it, and Paul had always been there for him. Tom

THE FINAL ACT

hadn't been afraid of putting the finger on Mabley and Costello for being dealers, agreeing with Paul that letting the courts handle them was the best way.

But the court system had failed him, Tom now decided. Somehow, Mabley and Costello had beat the system and were out on the street again, as if nothing had happened. He didn't mind them coming after him; he could handle that. But he did mind them going after Jimmy. Jimmy was a good guy and didn't deserve to get another concussion.

He fought to keep out of his mind his mother's dying words a few months before. "Don't hate, Tom," she'd told him. "Always forgive."

He'd tried hard not to hate Steve Schmidt, who had driven the car that knocked his mother down. It was harder not to hate Mabley and Costello. With Steve, it had been an accident. With the two drug traffickers, it was intentional. They'd sent four goons after him and Jimmy and had done their worst. They'd planted cocaine on Tom to try and get him put away in prison, and Tom figured they'd get someone in prison to go after him with a knife, the way Tom's father, trying only to break up a fight, had been killed in Joliet prison by someone with a screwdriver. *Mabley and Costello would get some con to take care of me*, Tom thought.

It was them or him. No matter what the cops or Paul or the detective talking to him were going to do about it. All Tom could think of was Jimmy, lying unconscious in the hospital, and it made him want to break out of the police station and go to him.

Damn, damn, damn!, Tom thought hopelessly, driving his right fist into the palm of his left hand, He'd never felt so helpless and trapped in his life.

8

Tom was even more worn out after another hour of going over his story again and again to Ward and other detectives who came into the small hotbox of a room. He hadn't had any sleep at all, and it was a little after six in the morning. His neck ached worse than it ever had before. He figured that fighting off Mabley's and Costello's goons had brought back an old boxing injury. Whatever it was, he was hardly able to think, the stabbing pain was so great in the back of his neck.

Ward tried to keep control of the interrogation, and Tom felt he was being fair. But other dicks kept coming in and trying their tricks on him. Finally, Tom couldn't take it anymore and he lowered his head and wouldn't answer any more questions. He'd told them the same thing over and over and still they didn't believe that it had all been a setup.

Someone came up behind Tom and grabbed a fistful of his hair. He felt his head being yanked back so hard, lightning seemed to shoot up the back of his head.

Just then the door opened again and, though Tom couldn't see who had come in because pain had clouded over his vision, he recognized Paul Maggiore's voice. Vaguely, he heard Paul talk to the detectives. He heard him call Ward by his first name several times. They knew each other, Tom realized. Good. Maybe now they would get somewhere.

Still, Tom could no longer think clearly. He needed some sleep. He needed the pain in his neck to stop.

It didn't take Paul long to talk everyone into leaving Tom alone in the room with just him and Ward. Then Paul pulled a chair up to Tom and asked him if he could just go over it one more time, for him.

Tom shook his head, looked at Paul, and wasn't sure if he was going to laugh or cry. Somehow, he got his story out again.

Paul hadn't known about Tom and Jimmy working at the center that night. He explained to Ward that he could vouch for everything else Tom had told him about how Mabley and Costello were after Tom. A quick phone call to Joe Grogan could prove Tom was telling the truth about where he and Jimmy had been until four o'clock that morning.

Paul found Grogan's home phone number in his address and telephone book and called him. Grogan verified that Tom and Jimmy had arrived at the center at a quarter to twelve, and agreed to work until four o'clock. He believed them when they said they'd worked the full shift, but said that he couldn't swear to it because he left shortly after midnight.

Tom suggested Grogan check with Earl Spencer. He didn't know the name of the woman volunteer they'd worked with until four o'clock. Paul asked the favor of Grogan and he complied. He found Earl Spencer's number and gave it to Paul. Paul called the number, woke Spencer out of a sound sleep to ask him about Tom and Jimmy having worked with him until four, and Spencer said that was right. To make sure Ward believed it, Paul had Spencer tell it directly to Ward.

THE FINAL ACT   71

Ward hung up the phone after talking to Spencer and studied Tom.

"It seems to fit," Ward finally admitted. "I just had to be darned sure. It accounts for why you and Jimmy Ryan were on the street at four in the morning, and why Mabley and Costello were out to get you. They *could* have planted the coke on you."

Tom couldn't believe the detective. Ward still didn't sound as if he believed him.

Finally, Ward said he'd talk to the lieutenant on duty and see if he would decide to let Tom go or not. Paul asked to be let in on their talk, but Ward said he preferred they talk by themselves. Afterward, Paul could put in a good word for Tom.

While they waited and talked some more together in the interrogation room, Joe Grogan came in. Paul hadn't expected him and was glad to see him. Tom was, too.

Paul filled Grogan in on what had happened. Grogan looked at Tom and Tom saw that he believed his story. Tom figured it was probably because Grogan knew Paul so well and trusted his judgment. Whatever the reason, Tom felt relieved that Grogan was also on his side and it made him like the guy even more.

Nearly half an hour passed before Ward returned with a young black officer whom Tom thought was probably new to the job of lieutenant. He shook hands with Paul, then was introduced to Grogan, and they talked for several minutes, going over most of it again. Finally, the lieutenant looked at Paul.

"He's yours," the officer said, then left the room.

Paul arranged it so the incident would not be put on the record. The police kept the coke and let Tom go, but only in trade for Tom's cooperation.

"We don't really care all that much about you," Ward admitted when they were alone again with just Paul and Grogan. "It's whoever's dealing the stuff we're after, and it does look like that's Mabley and Costello."

Tom wasn't sure he could cooperate with Ward on going after Mabley and Costello a second time. Maybe they'd arrest them again, but how long would they be put away? They'd just pay somebody off again and be back out on the street.

He had to agree with Ward, though. He knew he'd have to go along with him, if he was to be let go. But what did Ward have in mind for him? What did he mean by "cooperation"?

Tom could guess. He'd be used as a decoy. He'd be free to go his way, but when Mabley and Costello found out about it, they'd try to get at him again. They'd probably not get him beat up and plant drugs on him again. They'd go after him for good the next time. They'd be out to kill him.

It was what Tom had expected all along. And it was him or them, he'd decided, for what they'd done to Jimmy.

"Just let us know, or Paul," Ward told Tom, "if you run into Mabley or Costello or get any handle on what they're doing or where they are. For your own sake, we're going to have you tailed. It won't be the same plainclothesman all the time, but he won't get in your way."

"How am I going to know if it's a cop or some goon on my tail?" Tom asked.

Ward just cautioned Tom to be careful. Tom knew he'd have to be, from then on. He walked out of the station with Paul and Grogan and found that it had stopped raining. His shirt was more off than on, and his neck still hurt, yet it felt good to be free again. It probably wouldn't have happened, if not for Paul and Joe.

Joe went on his way and Paul drove Tom to Grant Hospital. He learned that Jimmy had been admitted and was resting

THE FINAL ACT

in a room on the fourth floor. He was conscious and was not badly hurt. Tom could hardly believe the good news.

Ellie and Marty were waiting outside Jimmy's room when Tom and Paul arrived. Mark Hawley was just coming out of the room and assured Tom that Jimmy was going to be okay.

"He took some head blows, but he must have given about as good as he got," the young hospital aide explained.

Tom was allowed to talk to Jimmy and went in by himself. He found his friend in bed as he'd expected, his head bandaged and propped up on pillows.

Jimmy laughed at the sight of Tom, his face red from bruises, his shirt half torn off.

"Lynch always said you were still a street fighter," Jimmy joked.

Tom pulled up a chair beside the bed, glad that Jimmy sounded like his old self.

9

Jimmy had to remain in the hospital for a few days, for tests and observation and rest. Tom wished his friend could be with him when he went back for more training sessions at the suicide prevention center, but he didn't let that keep him from going. He kept remembering the phone call from the girl with the broken heart and began to realize there were lots of other people out there who needed someone to talk to.

On Sunday, after just a few hours' sleep, he went to Marty's gymnastics meet and cheered the loudest when she won the all-around individual prize, which also helped her high school team to win the exhibition meet.

He went to a little party at her place that evening, after attending another training session in the afternoon. Ellie went to visit Jimmy in the hospital instead of coming to the party. Their roommate, Karen, wasn't there. Marty said she and Ellie hadn't seen her since the previous afternoon.

"She started telling us about a new boy she'd met and liked," Marty told Tom. "I think maybe she's at his place."

Tom thought he got the picture. "Maybe you ought to

think of putting up another card in the supermarket for a new roommate," he said with a smile. "I think *she's* found one."

"She *was* kind of spooky," Marty admitted, handing Tom a Coke. About a dozen young people crowded into her living room having soft drinks, pretzels, popcorn, and cheese and crackers. Soft rock played over the din of a lot of conversations going at the same time. "Listen to me! I'm already thinking of Karen in the past tense, as if she's already moved out. Well, she was hardly here, even when she was in the apartment. She never talked to us, except to ask a question about something or tell us she was going out. And I told her I really thought she ought to see a doctor. She shouldn't be on any kind of a diet, unless it's one to make her eat more and put some weight on her."

"I never saw anybody so skinny," Tom agreed. "Just skin and bones. Maybe she's got some disease that's wasting her away."

"She wasn't always that thin," Marty told him. "She showed us some pictures in her wallet. Just six months ago or so, she looked like she was of normal weight for her height. She had a good figure, in fact. But you'd never know it, from how she's changed."

"She didn't say what made her lose so much weight?"

Marty nodded that the girl hadn't confided in her or Ellie. "She just says meat and potatoes and most of the things we all eat are bad for us. She believes in macrobiotics—health food that is mainly grains and beans. She got me to eat some of it once last week and to me it tasted like shredded cardboard. And it just laid in my stomach like lumps of coal. Tasteless and bland, and very heavy."

"Well, maybe it'll be good if she doesn't come back," he said.

"She didn't bring much with her, and even that's not here anymore," Marty realized. "Maybe she won't come back.

THE FINAL ACT

She paid us her share of the rent and utilities in advance, so we won't get stuck. We'll wait a few days and see if she comes back or calls us. But in a way, I wish she would come back. I'm kind of worried about her. She needs help, not only about how thin she is, but there must be a lot of things troubling her. She looks like about the most unhappy kid I've ever seen."

Tom needed to change the conversation. He just wanted to be alone with his girl. They hadn't seen that much of each other lately, with him looking for work and her practicing for her gym meet. Now that she'd won, she could relax for a while. He hoped she'd want to do her relaxing with him.

They stood close to each other in the middle of the crowded living room. She liked how dressed up he was, and told him as she raised a hand to push a shock of hair off his forehead. He'd let it fall there to help cover the small bandage he'd put over the cut above his left eye.

He'd gotten a few hours' sleep and then showered and got dressed up for her party. He wore beige slacks and navy blazer, with a blue shirt and yellow-and-blue striped tie.

"I've never seen you so dressed up before," she teased.

He thought she looked dressed up too, in a lightweight summer dress with flowers printed all over it. Its elasticized neckline showed off her neck and throat. Her auburn hair fell nearly to her shoulders and he thought she never looked more beautiful or desirable.

"No blue jeans." She laughed, meaning both of them had forsaken Levi's that night.

"We're both out of 'uniform,' " he replied.

He liked her in jeans, but liked her better in a dress. She sure looked feminine to him that night. As usual, she wore no makeup, or almost none. She was a natural beauty and let it show. He knew lots of girls thought they would attract a guy more if they looked flashy. He thought girls who wore a lot of makeup looked cheap. And he also thought it was a waste of time and money. Any girl who spent that much time on her face and fingernails must be self-centered, or insecure. Most of all, he never thought he could kiss a face that had all that cream and rouge and lipstick on it.

He wanted to kiss Marty's face just then and did. Then he found a place to put down his drink, took her slim waist in his hands, and drew her to him. They kissed again, but when he wanted more, she resisted.

He got the message. She still didn't want them to get too heavy. It wasn't because they weren't alone, he could tell, it was just how she felt.

Tom felt very frustrated. He wanted Marty more all the time, but she continued to put the brakes on. He needed to talk to her about it, and to kiss her some more.

When he took her by her hand and began to lead her through the crowd and toward her bedroom, she hesitated for a moment, but when she saw how important it was to him, she followed.

He closed the door once they were alone in her room but she remained standing when Tom sat on her bed. He knew she hadn't agreed to come in there to make love. She'd agreed so they could finally talk about something he'd wanted to talk about almost since he first met her nearly six months before.

"I don't want us to get so serious, Tom," she insisted. "If we did, I might not be able to resist you. I've got to keep myself free, to finish high school, go to college, work up to the Olympics in a few years, and then there are some other goals I've been thinking about. I have so much to do before I can think of getting serious. Even with someone who means as much to me as you."

That was something, Tom thought. But it didn't help that much. Yet, another side of him understood what she was

THE FINAL ACT

saying. He knew how far he was from being able to think about getting married. He knew Marty wasn't the kind of girl who would agree to living together unmarried. She'd told him how she felt about that enough times.

She was right, but he hated to admit it. He was out of work and had to do some good thinking about his own future. He was almost eighteen but hadn't finished high school. He didn't think he could stand going back and completing his senior year.

Sitting on the edge of her bed, he looked at his girl and wondered how he was going to keep up with her. She was going to make it, he felt certain. She was the most determined person he'd ever met.

As if she knew what he was thinking, she told him she had some new ideas about what she wanted to do, too.

"More and more, I've been thinking I'd like to teach the physically handicapped," she confided, standing near him. "I'd need to get special training in physical therapy, so I could be qualified to help the handicapped. That's going to take more time and hard work."

He just had to hold her close. He got up and took her in his arms and she allowed that. He wished he could be as sure of his future as she was of hers. Marty knew where she was going and he envied that so much. He didn't know anyone who worked as hard about deciding on her future as she did, or anyone as determined to make her dream come true.

He knew she loved him, maybe even as much as he loved her. But the timing was wrong, for both of them. They both had too much to do before they could think of having a life together.

He still thought it could work, if they just lived together and didn't marry. He took a deep breath and asked her.

Marty drew away from him and went to the window in her room and looked out. He didn't follow her there.

"I don't go for that kind of thing," she admitted. "I think it's not only wrong, but it's why there are so many divorces and so many broken families and kids who are hurting inside. A lot of people sleep together, but I don't think they have the commitment to each other that has to be there if they're going to make a relationship last a lifetime."

He tried to convince her that he wasn't like that, that he felt a stronger commitment toward her than he ever expected would be possible for him to feel.

She turned at the window and looked at him patiently and lovingly.

"We could help each other," Tom insisted. "Married or not, it wouldn't matter. We both have a lot we want to do with our lives. That's fine. So we can help each other achieve our goals, our dreams. It would be easier, if we do things together."

She knew how easy and comfortable that sounded, but said at least one of them had to be realistic. If he couldn't be, she had to. She said she did love him, but it still wouldn't change her mind.

It wasn't because she was afraid of being tied down, she insisted. He'd challenged her with that before. And she even denied it, when he said maybe she didn't love him enough, or as much as he loved her.

"Where would we go on our honeymoon?" she said jokingly, looking at him from the window. "Oak Street beach?"

He laughed, but knew what she meant. Together, they had enough money to travel about two miles.

"You know where I've always thought I'd like to go on my honeymoon?" she asked. "China!"

It reminded him of his own honeymoon dream. "I've always thought I'd like to go to the Matterhorn in Switzerland—that big snowcapped mountain you see on lots of picture calendars. I've always wanted to go there and drink a can of beer at the bottom of the Matterhorn. Not climb it, just drink a beer at the base of it."

It made them both laugh and she walked over to where he was standing near her bed. "Tommy," she sighed, taking his troubled face in her hands and kissing him. "What I'm afraid of is, in China or in Switzerland or here in Chicago, if we lived together, I don't think I could handle it. I would want us to be as happy together as we could be, and that would mean sleeping together. I just can't take that chance. I might not be able to resist you, and that would hurt you even more."

He felt a little better, hearing that. It meant she wanted him as much as he wanted her. But he could see how hopeless it was, she was so strong against them living together, even unmarried.

A last-ditch thought came to him. "We could live together as roommates, like you and Ellie," he pleaded desperately, seeing that she was drifting away from him again, inside herself.

She kissed him again, then held him at arms' length. "Tommy, get serious," she said with a slight smile, looking into his deep blue eyes. "How do you think we could ever manage that?"

It became funny to him, too. How could he ever expect to room with Marty and treat her like his sister?

Marty reached out for his hand as she turned for the door. He took her hand, she opened the door, and they drifted out into the party, but he was no longer laughing.

Seeing all the other girls in the room in jeans and sweaters, with too much makeup on, Tom realized again what he had by the hand. Marty had class; it was one of the things he liked most about her. And he even began to respect her for not agreeing to go to bed with him.

10

The next week nearly flew by. Tom finished his training sessions at the suicide center and Jimmy got released from the hospital. He was on doctor's orders to rest at home for at least a week, so he didn't go to the center with Tom. But he promised he'd make up the training soon as he could and join Tom again as a volunteer.

Karen never showed up again at Marty's and Ellie's place. They figured she split for good and advertised for a new roommate. Tom jokingly called Marty and applied but wasn't surprised when she turned him down. By week's end, the girls were still looking for a replacement for Karen, to help with rent and other bills.

When Tom wasn't working two shifts at the center or filling in for other volunteers when they couldn't make theirs, he was checking the want ads and making calls on employment offices everywhere he could. The best he found was an occasional odd job for a few hours and a few dollars. To burn off some nervous energy, he worked out at the gym more frequently, sparring with whomever he could find.

All week, he kept on his guard for any sign of Mabley or Costello or anyone they might have hired to go after him. Once, he saw the blond guy who ran errands for them. He was coming out of another apartment building along Sheridan Road near Belmont Avenue and got into a waiting cab and drove off. Tom was on his way to the center again and couldn't follow. Somehow, he hadn't found time to go to where he was sure the guy lived and have the talk he wanted to have with him.

On Friday afternoon, coming home from a shift at the center, driving along Clark Street near Wrigley Field, Tom saw a girl he thought he recognized. She was in jeans and sleeveless shirt, but it was her skinniness that made him look closer. He didn't stop the car, just drove slowly behind Karen for a little while, and watched as she went into the lobby of a small apartment building. He parked nearby and waited. After about ten minutes, she came back out, putting her wallet in her purse. He thought she was probably on Mabley's and Costello's payroll as a delivery girl, just as the blond guy was one of their delivery boys, dealing look-alikes or other drugs for them.

She hailed a passing taxi and after the cab drove off, Tom made an illegal U-turn and followed. For some reason he wasn't too surprised when the cab pulled up and stopped in front of the four-story apartment building a few blocks away on Fremont, where Tom figured the blond guy lived. She paid the cab driver, then walked quickly up to the building and into the lobby. Tom thought about it a moment, then began driving home.

Tom figured Karen and the blond guy had been thrown together, working for Mabley and Costello. That was no surprise. Karen moved out on Marty and Ellie and probably had moved in with the blond guy. *Well*, he thought ruefully as

THE FINAL ACT 85

he drove back to the warehouse and his friends, *probably they were sleeping together*. He was glad some people were.

Jimmy was feeling well enough that night so they could all have a pizza party together at The Hot Spot. Marty and Ellie met Tom and Jimmy and the rest of the gang there. When he had a chance, Tom told Marty he'd seen Karen and figured she was living with the dealer he then told her about. She didn't seem interested in Karen or the blond guy, but when she learned more from him about Mabley and Costello, she became afraid for him.

He told her not to worry; a cop was tailing him all the time. Yet, Tom never did see anyone tailing him. He figured whoever was watching him was a pretty good undercover cop.

Saturday afternoon, Tom worked another four hours at the suicide center. He had a date with Marty for that night; it would be just the two of them, dinner at her place while Ellie and Jimmy went to a movie. Then Tom and Marty would go to a show at an amateur improvisational comedy place in Old Town. Tom hadn't seen any live entertainment in a long time, and this wouldn't cost much. On his budget, he had to be careful.

But before he left the center at five o'clock, Joe Grogan asked if he could do him a special favor and fill in for a volunteer who couldn't make his midnight-to-four-a.m. shift. That would make him cut his date with Marty shorter than he wanted to, but Tom agreed. He wanted to be as helpful as he could at the center and also figured he owed Joe, for how Grogan had stood up for him with the police the week before.

He'd never had a dinner alone with her that she had prepared. She and Ellie had worked up a couple of meals for him and Jimmy since they began sharing the apartment, but this was Marty's first time as solo cook and, Tom didn't know why, he was surprised at how good she was. They had baked stuffed pork chops with spicy dressing inside, Spanish rice, and a mixed salad. He brought a bottle of nonalcoholic wine that a liquor store clerk assured him was good though inexpensive. Tom had tried to talk the clerk into selling him some regular wine even though he was underage. The clerk held fast and assured Tom he'd hardly know the difference when he drank the Catawba.

Tom poured the light, dry white wine into Marty's tall-stemmed glass at her table and liked the look of it. They clinked glasses by candlelight, she in a soft green dress and he in tan sportcoat and knit tie, and he took a sip and liked the taste, too. It was from a reddish grape from a New York State vineyard, he told her, pretending to be a lot more knowledgeable about wines than he really was.

They finished dinner and he helped her do the dishes, then they sat on the couch in the living room and listened to soft music. He put an arm around her. She leaned her head on his shoulder and he knew she would be content to remain that way all evening. He wasn't content, however. He kissed her, and she returned the kiss. He began kissing her more and harder, and she pulled away and got up abruptly.

"I've been curious," she said, going to the stereo. "About Karen."

She didn't want to talk to him about getting it on heavy again, he knew. She needed something else to talk about and he understood.

"I told you, I think she's living with that blond guy from Colorado."

"I know," she said. "I mean, I was wondering about why she's so thin and on such a strict diet. I talked to my coach about it . . . Mrs. Sheridan. She says Karen sounds like she's anorexic."

THE FINAL ACT

Tom sat up, wondering if he heard her right. "Ana what?"

"Anorexia nervosa," Marty told him. "What they think Karen Carpenter died of. Some girls, and guys, too, just about starve themselves to death, on purpose."

He'd heard something about it but hadn't ever really known that much about it. Vaguely he remembered reading that the young singer had died of cardiac arrest, which probably had been brought on by self-starvation.

"Most girls are afraid they'll get fat," Marty explained. "I am too, I guess," she admitted, though she half-laughed. "But I exercise a lot, so I can put away a meal like tonight and it doesn't show. I know a couple of girls who starve themselves, then they're so hungry they gorge themselves on food, and then make themselves throw up afterward, for fear they'll gain weight. That's called bulimia. Karen McCauley may do that, too, but she didn't while Ellie or I were here. I think she is anorexic, though, from what I've heard about it."

Marty explained that anorexics have an irrational fear of being overweight, and it brings on compulsive dieting. Everything girls wear are made for slim figures. Especially jeans. So lots of girls will do anything, even starve themselves, in order to fit into the smallest pair of jeans they can.

"It starts in many different ways. Karen's father or mother may have kidded her that she was snacking too much and was getting fat. Her boyfriend might have told her she was putting on some weight. Her friends may have all agreed to go on a strict diet, to lose pounds and inches. She may have tried on a pair of jeans she wanted and found she couldn't breathe in them. So she made up her mind to stop eating."

Then it gets out of hand, Marty explained. The girl starts to equate losing weight and not eating with her own self-esteem. To gain even a pound is like being a moral failure. To lose another pound is a personal victory. When they're hungry enough, they gorge themselves, then induce vomiting, so they cure their hunger but do not gain the calories.

"After a while, the anorexic loses all self-control and no longer realizes how dangerous their self-starvation could be. Even after they've gotten down to only seventy-five or eighty pounds, they may still see themselves as being overweight and refuse to eat. About five to ten percent of anorexics die from self-starvation. It's supposed to be a regular epidemic among girls today in this country. Most guys aren't into it because the pressures aren't on them as much to be so thin. With guys, the pressure can be to put on weight, to lift weights, and be macho-looking. With girls, it's the opposite. The smaller, thinner, the better."

Tom was glad Marty hadn't any such crazy notions about being skinny. She looked just right to him, and she was the healthiest-looking girl he'd ever known.

"Some doctors and psychiatrists think the main cause of anorexia is that a girl is reluctant to grow up," Marty said. "Or they may be sexually immature. Or they may just starve themselves to get back at their mother for being so dominating."

Girls don't have it so easy, Tom decided. He was starting to realize what they had to do to look good and become date bait. Some of them really worked hard at it, either wearing a lot of makeup, or starving themselves to death. *What for?* he wondered. Why don't they just be themselves?

"How do they pull out of it?" Tom asked.

"First they have to face the fact that they are anorexic," Marty said. "Sort of like someone has to admit he's an alcoholic. There are support groups and treatment centers around. Mrs. Sheridan says treatment isn't easy and takes a while. The girl needs psychotherapy and her family has to be in on it too, so the causes of the malnutrition can be found out. Treatment might take as long as two or three years, but the only alternative is starving to death."

"And you think that's what Karen McCauley is doing?"

"What do you think? You saw her once, didn't you?"

He hardly remembered her face, except that he thought she was kind of pretty, though very young-looking. He did remember thinking she looked awfully skinny, both when he'd first seen her in the apartment and later on the street. He agreed that he did think Karen was a lot skinnier than she ought to be.

He began to laugh and Marty wondered how the serious conversation they were having could be funny to him.

"All this talk about not eating has made me hungry," he said, laughing self-consciously. "I've been wondering . . . did you make a dessert?"

11

During the days that followed, Jimmy was well enough to complete his volunteer work training and began manning the phones at the center with Tom. Each time Tom picked up a call there, he wondered if the caller would be the girl he'd talked to his first night as a volunteer, but she never called back. Instead, he took calls from people of all ages and he began to feel as if he was becoming a better listener. His own worries, about being out of work for nearly a month, were nothing, he realized, compared to what most of the callers laid on him.

One thing was helping, however. Tom found a few hours' work on weekdays helping a handyman-plumber when he needed some strong young arms to help him rod out sewers and catch basins. It was sweaty, dirty work but he needed the money, and he felt better about working at anything again. A few times he had to lower himself down into a catch basin full of mucky water and empty it, bucket by bucket, to drain it before a broken sewer pipe could be repaired or a clogged drain could be opened. It made Tom decide against being a plumber for sure and he became all the more eager to get back to being a carpenter.

The twenty bucks or more he got from each job helped a lot to keep things going at the loft. Maury and the other guys brought in what they could and they all pooled their money, but Tom had felt bad for weeks, not being able to pitch in. The sewer work helped him feel better.

Sometimes, Tom felt he was being followed, or checked on. He figured it was some undercover cop that the narcotics detective, Alvin Ward, had assigned to him. But it could also be someone Mabley or Costello told to tail him. He was still waiting for the other shoe to drop.

Toward the end of that week, when Tom and Jimmy got off the midnight shift at the center and sat having a Coke at an all-night restaurant near the warehouse, the blond guy came in. He recognized them and came over to their booth. He looked as if he didn't intend to butt in on them, if they didn't want him to, but Tom was glad for their chance meeting. He asked him to join them and he sat down next to Jimmy, across the table from Tom.

Tom had thought the guy was very good-looking the first time he'd seen him, nearly a month before at Belmont Harbor with Mabley. He still had his head of blond curls and still dressed like a rodeo rider, in gray twill slacks and blue satin western shirt with gray piping on the shoulders and pockets and down the front. But his eyes looked dark and his face was pale. *He'd lost some weight, too,* Tom thought. He couldn't remember ever seeing anyone change so much, in just about a month.

Introducing himself as Jeff Larsen, he took a half-empty pack of cigarettes out of a shirt pocket and lit up. Even from where he sat across from him, Tom could smell that Jeff was a heavy smoker. The fingers he used to hold his cigarette were stained yellow from nicotine, and he began coughing.

From his last name, Tom figured he was of Scandinavian descent. He'd heard that most Norwegians or Swedes were blond and often good-looking. Jeff sure had been, Tom remembered, thinking he reminded him of Chris Atkins. He still looked vaguely like the handsome young actor, but nowhere near as healthy as he'd looked before. Tom figured he was probably blowing the money he got from Mabley on drinking and drugs and having himself a pretty wild time living with Karen. Or maybe he'd kicked her out of his apartment by now and found someone new with whom to live. If so, he felt even more sorry and concerned about Karen McCauley.

Tom had become good at listening and being able to draw people out so they would open up and talk. It had worked pretty well over the telephone, but Tom was surprised how easy it was to get Jeff to open up to him and Jimmy as they sat together in the booth. Jeff ordered black coffee and started right in talking about himself.

He was seventeen but looked older. He'd split from his father who ran a small feed corn farm in Colorado on the eastern slope of the Rocky Mountains about fifty miles north of Denver. Jeff had grown up on small farms like that and helped his father, but when his mother ran out on them about a year before, things started going downhill for them. His father began drinking hard and almost never said anything, to Jeff or anyone.

"It got so spooky, I had to get the hell away from home," Jeff told them. "He was like a goddamn zombie."

It was severe depression, Tom knew. His own father when he'd drunk a lot never said a word to anyone. He would just sit in front of the tv set with a drink and look like he was in a trance. It often gave Tom the creeps.

"He's withdrawn inside himself," Tom told Jeff. "My dad was the same way. One day, he just exploded. He robbed a small savings and loan and got caught and put in prison. A few months ago he tried to break up a fight between some cons and got killed. A screwdriver in the back.''

Tom wasn't sure why he confided all that to Jeff. Maybe he wanted to prove to him that he'd had a rough time of it with his own father.

Jeff looked at Tom in a way Tom hadn't expected. Somehow, Tom had the feeling Jeff wanted to be his friend. The look in his almost frightened eyes, the slight break of a smile on his face, gave him away. Tom remembered how Jeff had seemed to want to get to know him and Jimmy before, when they'd bumped into each other outside another neighborhood restaurant shortly after they'd first met. But Tom hadn't wanted to talk to him then and brushed him off.

What he is, is damn lonely, Tom began to realize. He knew the look of a lonely person and the feel of it. He'd been there enough himself.

No wonder Jeff looked like he'd fallen apart, in only about a month, Tom decided. He'd run away from home and went from a farm to one of the biggest cities in the country, but knew no one here. He probably ran out of money fast and was desperate. Mabley or Costello came along and promised him plenty of money just to deliver stuff for them. Maybe Jeff didn't even know he was pushing drugs. More likely he did, but had no choice. It was a matter of surviving that way or living off the streets. Jeff didn't look like the kind of guy who would take his money that way, from some pervert who liked boys instead of girls. There was a lot of that going on around them, but Tom didn't think Jeff would ever get into it, no matter how desperate he was.

"We both know Mabley," Tom told Jeff, "and his partner, Costello. They're about the lowest couple of losers we've ever run into. They were pushing look-alikes when we got mixed up with them."

THE FINAL ACT

Tom explained that Maury had gone to work for them and later Tom had infiltrated Mabley's racket by pretending to work for him. That led to him learning that Costello was a narcotics detective who was using his knowledge about raids to tip off Mabley, teaming up to run a pretty safe drug business. Until Tom and his probation officer, Paul, were able to blow the whistle on them both and break up their racket.

"It was because they nearly killed my girl," Tom explained. "She took some of the look-alikes and nearly died."

Jeff set his coffee down and put out his cigarette, then immediately lit up another.

"I knew most of that, but thanks for telling it all to me," Jeff admitted. "Mabley told me, just after I went to work for him. I'm not with him or Costello anymore. I quit about a week ago. I saved most of what I got from them, but with rent to pay and other things, I'm about broke now. And I've got this girl living with me. She's a nice kid, even if she's skinny as hell."

Tom said he knew Karen, though only slightly. He told Jeff he and Jimmy had seen her enter his building a few weeks before, and he had recognized her as the girl who had been rooming with his sister and girlfriend for a short time. They were all worried about her because she was so skinny. When Tom told Jeff he and Marty believed Karen was anorexic, Jeff looked surprised. He hadn't heard about the illness and listened when Tom explained about it.

"I can't get her to eat anything anymore," Jeff said dejectedly. "I don't love her, but I couldn't tell her that. She seems to love me. I think it's just because she's so lonely. She's a runaway, too, but from a pretty well-off family in one of the suburbs."

It rang a bell in Tom's head. He couldn't remember from

where the girl who had called him that first night at HelpLine had said she'd come. He thought she said it was from a rich suburb of Chicago. *It could be the same girl*, he thought. But then he figured she wasn't the only teenage girl from a rich family in a Chicago suburb who had run away from home. The streets were probably full of them.

"You guys don't know of any work, do you?" Jeff asked, ordering another coffee. "I mean, I'll do just about *anything*."

"Don't settle for that," Tom cautioned, half-smiling. "There's always easy money around, but take it from someone who's been there, it isn't worth it. Jim-boy and I got laid off about a month ago. We were on a construction crew working for a real good guy. But the building business has been lousy, and he couldn't get enough jobs to keep us all busy so he laid us off. I was out of work for weeks but just got some part-time work helping a plumber work on sewers."

"I've done sewer work before," Jeff said. "Does he need another helper?"

Tom thought hard for a minute, looking at how desperate Jeff was.

"Tell you what," Tom said, wondering why he was going to say what he was. "I've got another offer coming up. So why don't you take my sewer job? I can talk to the guy and recommend you." He noticed the surprised look on Jimmy's face.

Jeff didn't look as if he believed Tom. "You're sure? You're not just saying that, because you feel sorry for me, being out of work and all? You really do have a new job offer?"

In spite of himself, Jeff was desperate to reach out for Tom's generous offer. Tom sensed that Jeff probably knew Tom was making it up about getting another job, but Jeff was

THE FINAL ACT

like a drowning man, reaching out for any kind of lifesaver. He knew he had made the right decision, helping the guy.

He offered his hand on it and Jeff shook it and thanked him until Tom was embarrassed. Tom caught the wink Jimmy gave him.

"Be careful, Tom," Jeff said then. "I was going to warn you anyway, before you told me about letting me have your job. Mabley and Costello . . . they're after you. You know they planted the cocaine on you. They wanted me to be in on that, but I said no way. It was that that made me decide to quit with them. They're probably after me, too, because I know too much."

Is that why he looks so bad? Tom wondered. It must be. Jeff's scared, and no wonder. Mabley probably threatened Jeff, too, with being bumped off and stuffed in the trunk of a car, if he quit or squealed to anybody about their racket.

"Maybe you ought to move in with Jimmy and me," Tom said, then explained to Jeff about the Guardians.

"It sounds great," Jeff said, picking up on Tom's second generous offer. "But what about Karen? Even if you'd let her come too, I doubt she would. She's pretty fouled up and scared. I think she's close to going off the deep end and taking an overdose of something, but she likes me so much, and depends on me to take care of her, she's holding on. I don't think she could handle moving in with you guys."

Jeff thanked Tom but said he thought that for Karen's sake, he'd better just keep the apartment and stay with her.

Jeff's decision made Tom feel more certain he'd done the right thing in giving up his job to him. Jeff wasn't a bad guy, as he'd thought at first. He was just lonely and scared and desperate, like a lot of others Tom knew. Like he himself had once been.

They traded short histories after that, and after Tom and

Jeff told a little more about themselves, Jimmy told Jeff about growing up in orphanages. Tom said the other Guardians had similar stories to tell. What it all added up to was too many divorces and broken families, too little money and too much drugs and alcohol, and pressures from every which way.

"All the reasons they give us at the center," Tom told Jeff, then explained about HelpLine. "Not that I'm worried about you," he said, jotting the phone number on a napkin and pushing it in front of Jeff. "But you never know. Maybe Karen might need to call it sometime."

It was nearly two o'clock in the morning when they decided to call it a night. Jeff left the restaurant with them and accepted the ride Tom offered, since he didn't have wheels anymore.

"Easy come, easy go," Jeff chuckled, when Tom let him out in front of his apartment building near Cubs' Park. "Two weeks ago, I was driving a new Audi. Now it's shank's mare."

"What?" Tom asked as he and Jimmy stood outside the car with Jeff.

"He means his legs," Jimmy explained, then he and Jeff laughed. He'd told Tom before that he'd spent a little time on a farm when he was just a kid.

Tom got the message and shook his head. "Well, *I'm* no farmer. I'm a city guy!"

12

Tom looked for another job after he gave up his sewer work but didn't find anything. He went back to punching the bag harder at the gym and spending more time at the suicide center. Slowly, Jimmy was going back to being his old self again. Before long, he was able to get in the ring and be Tom's sparring partner once more.

Paul talked to Tom at their Friday night Outreach volleyball game and asked if he was having any trouble with Mabley or Costello. Tom replied that he hadn't. He thought they might be laying low for a while, not wanting to risk getting caught again. But Paul still cautioned Tom to be on his guard.

A few days after Tom gave up his job to Jeff, he got a phone call from Ed Mrazek, the plumber. Jeff had called him to say he was quitting. He'd sounded both anxious and embarrassed, the man said. Tom couldn't figure it out, Jeff had needed work so badly. But Tom agreed to go back to helping the man with sewer work.

Tom went to Jeff's building twice and rang the bell in the hallway, but there was no answer. He'd tried both during the afternoon and at night. He left a message for Jeff to call him at the loft or at the center, and wrote down both phone numbers.

Spring turned warm, then hot. Tom worked shirtless with Ed Mrazek, a short but strongly built man in his late sixties, attaching lengths of coil to an electric sewer rodder to open a catch basin. It was dirty, sometimes frustrating work, but Tom was grateful for it and the money Mrazek paid him. He found he could talk to the man, too, and it felt better working for him again after he'd been able to explain to him about Jeff.

Mrazek said that explained why Jeff had always been looking around while they worked, as if he was afraid he'd see someone he didn't want to. Jeff knew that Mabley and Costello were after him, for quitting them. Nobody quit them and got away with it.

It was quite a load Jeff was carrying, Tom figured. He had his own thoughts about being a runaway, worrying about the drug goons being after him, and dealing with Karen McCauley and her anorexia.

A few nights later, Tom heard that the talk on the street was that Jeff had gone back to working for Mabley and Costello. Tom was certain it wasn't by choice. Jeff was all alone, except for Karen, and couldn't handle the threats from the dealers.

What could Tom do about it? Not much. It wouldn't do any good to try to talk Jeff out of working for them again. Not with Jeff's life on the line. All he could hope to do was be ready to help Jeff, when the time would come. And Tom figured that might not be far off.

A quiet week followed. Tom welcomed it. Too much had been going on with him and his friends. Too many downers.

THE FINAL ACT 101

His work with Ed Mrazek became more steady and even though he was often up to his waist in sewers, he was glad for the money he was earning. But it wasn't only that, he realized. It felt good to be busy again. The hours and days had dragged before. He'd had many sleepless nights while he was out of work and broke, now the time fairly flew by and he looked forward to each new day.

By mid-spring, everything around him was green or in bloom. He loved spring. It had been a long, rough winter in a lot of ways. Now he could breathe the fresh warm air and have a long summer to look forward to. It gave him a lot to think about.

He began planning a weekend bike trip, in Indiana or Michigan, that he and Marty and Jimmy and Ellie could take together. They could drive to a state park or wilderness area, then take a long bike and camping trip.

Ten-speed bikes were too expensive, but by luck, Tom found an older three-speed bike at a yard sale for only twenty-five dollars. It needed a new rim and tire, but he bought them and fixed the bike up like new. Then he read in the paper that a lot of unclaimed stolen bikes that the police had recovered were to be sold at a police auction. For practically nothing, Jimmy, Marty, and Ellie were able to buy bikes for themselves.

After that, every free evening and most of their weekends, the four of them took bike rides. They pedaled together to Lincoln Park Zoo, south to Hyde Park for an outdoor art fair, out to O'Hare airport to watch the jets take off and land, and west to the forest preserves to picnic and throw crackers at the ducks. It was a rare, wonderful time for them all. Jimmy's health quickly returned and Tom couldn't remember ever feeling so good.

Tom heard about some small lagoons far southwest on the

outskirts of the city where lots of wildfowl nested, and there were even some wild animals, including deer. They pedaled out there one Sunday morning and Tom was amazed by the area. It was like being up in the northwoods in some wilderness country, yet they were close enough to the city to see the tall skyscrapers in the Loop, far in the distance to the east.

He didn't know one bird from another, except for a redbreasted robin or a bluejay or cardinal. But there were plenty of ducks and he loved ducks. They were always interesting to watch, whether they were gliding smoothly on the surface of the water or flying down for a landing.

While Jimmy and Ellie were hiking up a trail, Tom and Marty sat on a grassy knoll beside one of the lagoons that had a lot of lily pads in the shallows. He took off his shirt and felt the warm rays of the sun on him and lay back on the grass. Marty lay beside him and they remained that way awhile, just holding hands, enjoying being side by side.

He rolled over and kissed her and she returned his kisses, and he drew her close to him and she didn't resist. He felt so good, he laughed, and lay back down on the grass again on his back. Marty played her hands through Tom's thick black hair and he closed his eyes. *It was good,* he thought, *very, very good.* He couldn't remember when life seemed better.

It didn't even spoil things for him, a little later when he tried unbuttoning her shirt.

"No, Tom," she cautioned, putting her hand on his. "Not too serious, remember?"

He moved a little way away from her and sat looking at the ducks with his arms holding his knees close to him so he rested his chin on them. She moved over beside him, stroked the side of his head, and neither of them said anything. He felt better in a minute or two, knowing she probably did feel the same about him as he felt about her. It just wasn't their time yet. For now, it was good enough. He looked at her and smiled and she kissed him and they went back to watching the ducks.

13

The next day was hot and muggy. Tom took his shirt off as he worked with Ed Mrazek on a sewer at an old house near Cubs' Park. Sweat poured off him as he was connecting sewer cables, and even with his back turned, he felt someone watching him.

He turned with a start and saw a big-shouldered man come into the backyard through an alley gate and walk toward him. He wore a blue T-shirt, tan golf jacket, and jeans, and Tom figured he got his muscles by way of wrestling or weight-lifting.

Tom dropped a length of sewer cable he was holding and picked up the shovel with which he had just finished digging a hole. Mrazek saw the man, then looked at Tom as he held up the shovel.

"It's okay, Tom," the man said as he came closer, taking a wallet out of his back pocket. "I'm a friend of Paul Maggiore's."

The man showed a police badge and identified himself as Wes Roeder.

"I'm with a stake-out and surveillance team," he explained. "I'll be hanging around for a while. I just wanted you to know, so you didn't think I was working for Mabley or Costello."

The undercover cop knew all about everything, Tom could tell. They didn't have to talk about it in front of Mrazek.

"We're expecting something to break real soon, with Mabley and Costello," Roeder told Tom, taking him aside so they wouldn't be overheard. "It involves a cocaine deal of some kind. But the word is out that they're ready to go after you. I don't want to tell you this to scare you, just to alert you."

Tom put the shovel down and began working again with the heavy iron sewer cable.

"They don't scare me," Tom told the cop. "I've handled them and a lot worse before."

Just the same, he was glad the cop had warned him and that he would be around, in case Tom needed him.

"How about that kid they've got working for them again," Tom said, more concerned than ever about Jeff. "A blond guy about my age."

"We're not after him," Roeder assured Tom. "We know how Mabley and Costello work, scaring kids into doing their dirty work for them. But, actually, we haven't seen the kid for the last week or so. Maybe he split."

Did Jeff go back to Colorado? Tom hoped he had. Maybe then Jeff would have a chance to shake Mabley and Costello off his trail. Did he take Karen with him? Tom made a mental note to check on Jeff and the girl again, after work that day.

He and Roeder shook hands and the cop let Tom get back to work. Ed Mrazek didn't ask any questions. Tom knew the old man liked and trusted him and if Tom didn't want to confide in him about what had gone on between him and the man, it was okay. Tom wished he could tell Mrazek about it all, but thought that for Mrazek's sake, he should leave him out of it. The less Mrazek was involved in this part of Tom's life, the better it would be for the old man.

After they finished on the sewer, at about five o'clock, Tom drove over to Jeff's building a few blocks away. He rang the bell, but there was no answer. He couldn't enter the building unless a tenant buzzed the lobby to open the inner door, so Tom began buzzing other people who lived there, but no one buzzed back. After a while, he gave up and left. Driving home, he wondered again if Jeff had gone back to Colorado. It would be the smartest thing he could do. But if Jeff had left town, did he take Karen with him? Tom decided that right after dinner, he'd check into it.

Jimmy took on the job of cook, since he still couldn't find even a part-time job. That night he made tacos and the guys all liked them. While Tom was enjoying thirds, the phone rang.

It was Joe Grogan calling to ask if Tom and Jimmy could work that night, though they weren't scheduled to. They were needed to fill in again on the midnight-to-four shift. Tom had hoped to see Marty that night, and to make it a late one, but he agreed to help out, and Jimmy volunteered, too.

Tom spent the early part of the evening with Marty and was glad she and Ellie hadn't decided on a new roommate yet. They were managing to pay the rent by themselves and liked not having a third girl around. So did Tom.

He and Jimmy drove over to Jeff's place before reporting to work at the center. Again, Tom found no one at home when he rang. Well, that was that, he figured. Jeff really must have moved away and left the city.

It was a relief to Tom, as he began to convince himself that that was what happened. The undercover cop, Roeder, thought the same. Jeff had gotten scared enough to split. Tom wished he could have talked to Jeff once more before he left, but he was glad he'd gone. He hoped Jeff had taken Karen with him. Maybe if Karen went along with Jeff to Colorado she'd get healthier on the fresh air and sunshine and start eating more. It could be the best thing for them both.

Earl Spencer was the only other volunteer on duty with them that night. Tom couldn't remember it ever being so quiet. There were no calls at all for the first hour and Tom smiled when he saw Jimmy falling asleep at his desk. He almost laughed; Jimmy sure wasn't a night owl.

Two calls came in at about one-thirty, almost on top of each other. Earl Spencer took the first one, Tom the second.

He recognized the caller right away, because she ended many of her sentences with, "You know what I mean?"

It was the poor little rich girl from the North Shore. He hadn't talked with her since his first night as a volunteer. He wondered if she'd called the center since then, but maybe one of the other people manning the phones had talked to her.

She sounded high on something and Tom could hardly make sense of what she was saying. She'd ramble on about her ex-boyfriend, then would change the subject, and he didn't catch half of what that was, before she would go back to talking about Floyd.

"Betty's really got her claws into him now," the girl said. "You know what I mean?"

Tom nearly laughed. He knew what she meant. He knew girls who knew their way around guys they wanted.

"They were living together, now she's pregnant," she told Tom. "She's like I am, sixteen. Oh, I don't care about them. I don't care about Floyd anymore. I've got my own guy now. He's fifty times better than Floyd. A hundred . . . two hundred. . . ."

THE FINAL ACT

Tom smothered a laugh. She was high, but she could still count. He wondered how high she was going to go, giving a score to her new boyfriend.

Suddenly, the girl began crying. She didn't say anything to Tom for several minutes, but he could hear her bawling uncontrollably. Then she hung up.

He waited anxiously but she didn't call back. It gave him a while to think about her situation. She obviously still carried the torch for Floyd, but he'd gotten his new girlfriend pregnant. Tom couldn't tell if the young couple intended on keeping the baby or going for an abortion. Either way, they had put a lot of pressure on themselves and the girl who had called, too. At least she had some new guy she was going with. He knew how it went. She sounded like she was still crazy about Floyd but had found somebody else to pick her up on the rebound, someone to whom she could transfer her love. At least this new guy was helping her to hold herself together as best she could.

Tom and Jimmy both handled a few calls in the final hour of their shift. Afterward, Tom looked at the big clock on the wall near the front door of the center and stretched and yawned. It was almost four o'clock and their replacements would be arriving at any minute. He was so tired he could hardly keep his eyes open, and Jimmy looked even more sleepy.

Two volunteers arrived, but just as Tom started away from his desk, his phone rang. He went back and got it and was not too surprised when he heard the girl's familiar voice again. She seemed even more anxious and upset.

"He's taken an overdose!" she cried into the phone, then left it.

Tom waited for the girl to return, so he could find out where she lived and he could call for paramedics to go there.

But the girl didn't come back to the phone. Faintly, Tom heard her calling to whoever had taken the overdose, and crying. He listened and tried to hear what was going on where she lived, but he couldn't get any clues.

With her phone off the cradle or hook, he couldn't get the operator to check the number. The girl had to come back to the phone and either tell him her address or hang up so he could call the operator.

More anxious moments passed and the other volunteers gathered around Tom at his desk, everyone, including Tom, feeling desperate and helpless.

Suddenly, Tom leaped out of his chair and handed the phone to Earl Spencer.

"She's calling to some guy at her place who's taken an overdose of something," Tom said excitedly. "She calls him Jeff. At least, that's what it sounds like."

He started for the door, then called back to Spencer as Jimmy followed him.

"I think I know who's taken the overdose and where he lives," Tom told the others. "It's near Cubs' Park on Fremont. I know the building but not the exact address. Maybe the girl will come back on the line and tell you what her address is. But don't wait. Call for paramedics. Send them to Fremont Street, a few doors north of Addison. My green VW will be parked outside the right building."

Tom hurried out of the center and Jimmy followed. As they approached the car, they saw someone lurking in the shadows at the back of the car, but when they began running toward him, the person took off.

"One of Mabley's and Costello's goons," Tom told Jimmy as they looked the car over quickly.

Tom lifted the hood on the back of the car and quickly checked out the engine as best he could without a flashlight. It didn't look tampered with, but he couldn't be sure.

THE FINAL ACT

Had the goon wired the car with a bomb? Tom thought he wouldn't put it past him.

"Don't get in, Jimmy," Tom cautioned. "Run up the block a ways. If it doesn't blow up, I'll pick you up."

Jimmy tried to talk Tom out of starting the car, but Tom wouldn't listen. He had to get over to Jeff's right away.

Tom held his breath and put the key in the ignition.

14

To his great relief, Tom heard the engine turn over and purr. He thought of himself as being a cat with maybe eight more lives to live.

He burned rubber going half a block to where Jimmy waited anxiously. The car was still in motion as Jimmy opened the door on the passenger side and got in.

Jimmy looked at his friend with disbelief. "Sometimes you scare the shit out of me!"

Tom chuckled as he pressed down on the gas pedal. "Sometimes I scare the shit out of myself!" he said seriously.

He figured that whoever had been hanging around the car hadn't had time to fool with it or plant a bomb. They'd scared him off. At least, for now.

Tom didn't think the old car had it in her. They got to the apartment building on Fremont so fast, he thought he could drive the Volkswagen at the Indy 500 that Memorial Day weekend.

They got out of the car but an idea suddenly came to Tom as he started for the building.

"Maybe, just to be on the safe side, you better wait here and make sure that goon doesn't do a number on the car yet," Tom told Jimmy. "If I need help upstairs, I'll call out the window for you. And you can tell the paramedics where to go, when they get here."

It made Tom feel good about his car, when he saw that they had even beaten the paramedics there.

Jimmy waited anxiously at the car while Tom entered the building and pressed the buzzer for Jeff's apartment. There was no answer and Tom's heart began pounding. He waited a moment, then leaned on the buzzer, but still no one opened the door.

It was about a quarter past four in the morning and everyone else in the building was probably sound asleep, but Tom had no choice. He punched the bell next to Jeff's. After more anxious waiting, he heard a man's voice coming out of a small speaker over the bell he'd punched.

"Who the hell is it?" the man asked, both sleepy and grouchy.

"It's the paramedics," Tom told the man. "Someone's taken an overdose in the building. Let us in."

"Get the hell away from here," the man's voice growled at Tom as he held his ear close to the receiver by the mailbox. "I'm not letting anybody in at four in the morning. Get away from here, or I'll call the cops. I think I'll call the cops anyway!"

Tom tried to talk to the man but he wasn't there anymore. Desperately, Tom pressed all the other bell buttons along the mailboxes on the wall in the entrance way. Soon other voices shouted at him from the mailboxes. Still, no one let him in.

After a few more minutes, Tom saw a paramedics ambulance pull up out front of the building. A moment later, he

THE FINAL ACT 115

heard the buzzer sound and grabbed for the door handle. He opened the door and was up the stairs before the paramedics.

Some tenants came out of their rooms in bathrobes and nightgowns, wondering what was going on.

"Where does a young guy named Jeff live?" Tom asked an old man who came to the stairs.

"Third floor, to the right," the elderly man replied. "What's . . . ?"

Tom didn't wait to explain. He took the stairs two at a time and called behind him for the paramedics to follow.

Tom found the door to Jeff's apartment locked when he tried the knob. He began pounding on the door but when there was no answer to his calls to Jeff, he tried breaking it open with his shoulder. Before he broke through, a man in a robe came up with a key and said he was the building's custodian.

Tom entered the apartment with two young paramedics, one black and one white. They found a girl face-down on the couch, her right arm hanging limp to the floor. Tom saw Jeff slumped in an easy chair, his head fallen to his chest. He was in tan twill pants, blue satin rodeo shirt, and boots. An open, empty bottle of pills lay on the floor nearby.

The medics went to work quickly and efficiently, checking out both Jeff and the girl. When she was turned over, Tom wasn't surprised to see it was Karen McCauley.

A lot began to make sense to Tom all at once as he watched the paramedics work. It had been Karen all the time. She was the girl who had called him at the suicide prevention center. She was the poor little rich girl from the North Shore who still carried a torch for Floyd. And Karen had found a new guy to live with—Jeff.

"Anorexia," Tom heard one medic tell the other as they lifted Karen off the couch and onto a stretcher.

The other medic phoned for another ambulance. "We've got two here," he reported to a fire station radio operator.

"The girl seems even worse off than the boy. We'll take the girl to Grant. Send another ambulance for the boy. Two drug overdoses."

Tom explained that he knew both Jeff and Karen and would stay and wait for the backup ambulance to come for Jeff.

"Are they both going to make it?" Tom asked anxiously as the medics began carrying Karen out.

"We'll do all we can," the black medic assured Tom. "Stay here, okay? Loosen his collar and belt."

Tom rested Jeff's head back, then opened his shirt and undid his wide leather belt. He talked softly, calling Jeff's name, but Jeff was out and showed no signs of responding.

Within minutes, Tom heard a siren approaching outside and, shortly after, another paramedics unit entered the apartment. The medics looked Jeff over, then took him out on a stretcher.

Tom and Jimmy followed the ambulance to Grant Hospital. When they got there, Tom forgot about the danger of someone tampering with his car, and so did Jimmy. They both entered the hospital and Tom left the car in a metered parking place on the street near the emergency entrance.

As Jeff and Karen were taken into separate curtained rooms, an admitting nurse began asking Tom questions about them. Medics had found a wallet on Jeff, but no identification on Karen. He told the nurse as much as he knew about both of them, then he and Jimmy sat on a bench and waited in a visitors' lounge just off the emergency room.

Tom looked up at a clock and saw that it was almost five o'clock. He was exhausted and could tell Jimmy was, too, seeing his friend lean back with his head against the wall, his eyes closed.

Tom remembered the car then, but didn't get up from the bench. It was too late to go check on it now. It had been

THE FINAL ACT

parked there for about half an hour. If someone wanted to fool with it, they sure had time. But he didn't think anyone would, because it was parked near the emergency entrance and people came and went around there all the time, including hospital guards and cops.

Tom hadn't realized that he had fallen asleep when someone awakened him. He and Jimmy had been so tired sitting and waiting that they slept sitting up for nearly an hour when a nurse gently shook Tom's shoulder. He and Jimmy both woke up.

"Your friend Jeff is conscious now," she said to Tom. "He's in serious condition from an overdose of barbiturates, but he's expected to recover. The girl, Karen, is more serious. She's terribly underweight and she had a bad reaction from taking some look-alike drugs containing very heavy doses of impure drugs."

"How are her chances?" Tom asked, rubbing his eyes.

"We'll know more in a few more hours," the nurse replied. "Why don't you leave your phone number and go home and get some rest? We can call you if there's any change."

Tom left his number and he and Jimmy left the hospital and walked to his car. With every step he took, Tom became more anxious about whether someone had planted a bomb this time. The sun was just coming up and Tom was glad it was lighter out. He didn't see anyone hanging around the car, but since he and Jimmy had been in the hospital nearly an hour and a half, anyone could have gotten to it.

He played the same trick as before, telling Jimmy to stand half a block away until he got the car started. He said a quick prayer, put the key in the ignition, turned on the engine, and heard nothing but its purr. Even more relieved than before, Tom drove up to Jimmy, he got in, and they drove home.

15

Tom slept the sleep of the dead. The other Guardians had been up, ate breakfast, and left for school or work before Tom and Jimmy awakened at about noon when the telephone rang.

A day nurse at the hospital told Tom that Jeff was responding well to treatment. He could receive visitors that afternoon. Karen, however, was still unconscious and being treated intravenously.

Tom took no chances on leaving the car outside; he opened the rear garage doors on the warehouse and drove the car inside. He would park it there overnight until he could be sure it would be safe, and only drive it in an emergency. He and Jimmy took a bus to the hospital that afternoon.

Jeff wasn't sitting up in bed when they arrived in his room, but Tom wasn't expecting him to be. Three others were in beds in the room, two older men and a boy with a broken leg. Tom hated hospitals, and it was too soon after his mother had died in that one. But he figured Jeff had no one else to visit him and he probably needed someone to talk to.

Jeff, it turned out, hardly said a word. He was still too weak and under medication. But he recognized Tom and Jimmy and his eyes told them he was glad they came. They talked to him, then, after only about ten minutes, they left, assuring him they'd come back that evening and often, until he was well enough to leave. Tom also told him that this time, he wouldn't let Jeff refuse his invitation. Jeff was to come live with Tom and the others in the loft.

Jeff asked them about Karen but they had no news for him about her. She was getting good treatment there and that was all they knew.

Jimmy went back to the loft and Tom took a bus to Ed Mrazek's and worked the rest of the afternoon. That evening, after dinner, Tom and Jimmy visited Jeff again.

This time when they entered his room, Jeff was sitting up in bed and looking more alert and alive.

"I can get out of here the day after tomorrow, with luck," he told them. "And I'll take you up on your offer. I've been told that Karen will be here longer, but she's expected to recover. That's a load off my mind."

It was good news to Tom and Jimmy, too.

"She can move back in with my sister and girlfriend," Tom told Jeff.

Tom didn't think it was the right time to tell Jeff about Karen's phone calls to the suicide center. Suicide was probably a subject Jeff didn't want to talk about, at least until he got out of the hospital. *Had he taken the barbiturate overdose intentionally?* Tom wondered. Had Jeff intended to take his own life? Tom wasn't sure about that, but now wasn't the time to find out about it.

"One thing's for sure," Jeff told them. "I'm through working for Mabley and Costello. They'll be after me again, but I don't care anymore. I've been scared long enough. I'm not going to be scared anymore."

THE FINAL ACT

Tom took Jeff's hand and shook it. "You're not alone." He half-laughed. "They're after me, too. So we'll just stick together, okay? We'll look out for each other. That's what the Guardians do. Everybody looks out for everybody else."

Jeff sounded tired and Tom and Jimmy left him, saying they would come back the next afternoon. Before leaving the hospital they checked on Karen's condition and learned she was conscious and starting to respond to treatment. But she was still not out of danger, mainly because she was so undernourished. She was being fed intravenously but that had to be done carefully because she had come dangerously close to starving herself to death.

Tom couldn't figure Karen. How could anyone want to starve themselves? He *loved* to eat! If he put on too many pounds, he worked them off with exercise, or pushed the plate away from himself, or ate half what he usually ate. He didn't *stop* eating. What was so beautiful about being so skinny that you didn't even cast a shadow? He liked some meat on his bones, and his girl's. He even wondered how a handsome guy like Jeff, so athletically built and healthy, looking like the all-American boy from Colorado, could have gone for a girl as skinny as Karen. He must have been pretty lonely or she must have some personality!

Jeff didn't look so handsome or healthy in his hospital bed, but Tom thought he caught a hint of life coming back to him. He wasn't going to work for the drug goons anymore; that was a very good sign. He'd done some thinking while he was in the hospital and was starting to pull himself together. Tom would get him over to the gym and into a pair of boxing gloves and teach him the ropes. Boxing could help restore Jeff's health, as it had Tom's.

Tom and Jimmy talked about all that and more an hour later while riding their bikes along the lakefront. It was a cloudless night and a lot of stars shone overhead, considering the city pollution and lights that usually hid the stars. It was a warm evening and they enjoyed the cooling breeze coming in from Lake Michigan. Tom had thought of inviting Marty and Ellie to go biking with them, but this was one of those times he preferred to be either alone or with his best friend.

Tom felt good, biking side by side along the retaining wall at Oak Street beach with Jimmy. Jimmy was always so easy to be with. They could talk or say nothing yet always feel tuned in to each other. Jimmy was more to Tom than a best friend or even a brother. *He was like an extension of himself,* Tom thought. They were like the Corsican Brothers from the famous novel and movie. Tom, the old movie nut, remembered the picture with Douglas Fairbanks, Jr. playing twins, each of them feeling the other's pain or love. He thought it was like that with him and Jimmy. They were like one person and always would be. Maybe it was because they had already been through so much together. It was that that made the bond between them so strong. They had shared good times and bad, fought each other, at least in the ring, and stood up for each other when they had been in danger. Just a year of knowing each other had turned into a lifetime of caring.

None of it had to be said, as they biked together, yet Tom knew Jimmy felt the same way. It was how best friends were.

As they biked north again around Belmont Harbor, car lights shone on them and Tom thought it might be someone sent out by Mabley or Costello. A voice called out from the car, but the headlights blinded them and they couldn't see who was behind the wheel in the darkness.

"It's me, Tom," a man's deep voice called. "It's Wes Roeder."

Tom and Jimmy stopped and the plainclothes cop leaned out of the window on the driver's side of his car.

"We heard about Jeff," Roeder said. "How's he doing?"

"Coming around," Tom reported. "The girl, Karen

McCauley, is, too, but it'll take her longer."

Roeder asked what Tom knew about them both and he told him as much as he knew.

"Jeff had his wallet on him," Roeder said. "His doctor called Jeff's father in Colorado. He'll be here tomorrow."

Tom said he wondered if that would do any good. Jeff had said his father was a drunk and wouldn't open up and talk, he kept everything inside himself. Well, maybe it was a good sign. Jeff's father was showing that at least he cared, enough to make the trip from Colorado to see his son in the hospital.

"I don't think Jeff will want to go back with him to their farm," Tom said. "If he doesn't, he's going to move in with us Guardians. Karen can go back to rooming with my sister and girlfriend."

"Sounds like a good setup, for both of them," Roeder said. "I'll have somebody look after Jeff, now he's quit Mabley and Costello again. Be careful, you guys. I'll be around."

They watched Roeder's car until it got lost in traffic and they biked back home. Tom had gotten into the habit of looking in the rearview mirror of the car when he drove. It transferred over into his bike riding and every little while as he pedaled, he would look behind him.

He wished it would all end soon. He hated living the way he was, wondering when the other shoe was going to drop. If the drug goons didn't make a move for him soon, he began thinking he'd go after them for a change.

It was like he felt while training for a boxing match, Tom decided. He always felt anxious, yet itching to mix it up, to get into the ring and touch gloves and come out fighting. He hated the waiting, the anticipating.

He knew what it was he hated. It was the uncertainty. How good would he be when the fight began? What shape would he be in and how good would his opponent be?

Tom always hated uncertainty, but he knew there was nothing you could do about it. Life wasn't a certain or sure thing. Every day could bring a surprise that could wipe you out or make you feel terrific.

He remembered what his mother had told him, the night she died. Take one day at a time. Put one foot in front of the other and before you know it, another day has come and gone and you've made it through the tough part. You've survived.

Even feeling like some of Mabley's and Costello's goons were lurking behind them in the dark as they pedaled their bikes home, Tom felt sure about one thing—he'd survive. He'd come through this like he'd come through everything else, and be the better and stronger for it.

Yet, what *was* that behind them as they pedaled into the alley behind the warehouse? A car was pulling out the other end of the alley. In the glow of the naked bulb over the warehouse door he thought the car was shiny and silvery. Like the Audi.

16

Tom hadn't expected trouble during the daytime. He expected Mabley and Costello or their muscle to do their dirty work under cover of darkness.

The following afternoon, after he'd visited Jeff for a while in the hospital, Tom met Ed Mrazek at another house for a sewer job. It was hot out, in the low 80s, and Tom felt the sweat pour off him as he worked shirtless and in dirty jeans, lifting bucket after bucket of smelly black water out of the sewer and dumping it into a metal garbage can.

A dog up the alley began barking as he had several times earlier when strangers passed the yard he was in. Tom looked up and saw two big guys get out of a car they had pulled up to the gate. He didn't recognize them by face but could tell what they did for a living.

"There's going to be trouble, Ed," Tom called out to the old man. "You better go inside the house."

Mrazek saw the men start to enter the yard and looked at Tom.

"I'll call the police," he said, then went up the back stairs of the house.

Tom set down his bucket of sewer water and picked up two lengths of heavy iron cable. It would be better than a shovel against two of them, he estimated. Unless they decided to use a gun on him, but somehow he didn't think that was in their plans. At least, not in broad daylight with Mrazek as a witness.

The two men were about the same size, both built like Sherman tanks from World War II. They wore short-sleeved knit shirts and jeans, so their biceps and pectoral muscles nearly popped out of the cloth. Tom had never seen boxers built like that. They were more like wrestlers or weightlifters. Whoever they were, they were huge.

"Put the cable down, sonny," one of them said, wiping his hands on the front of his blue shirt.

Tom held the cable more firmly and showed them what he could do with it, flinging it out like it was a whip.

The other goon, in a red shirt, laughed at Tom. "Put down the buggy whip, kid, or we'll take it away from you."

"Come and get it," Tom coaxed. Now he was really itching to get at it. He could almost hear the bell ring and pictured himself walking to the center of the ring and touching gloves with his opponent.

The guy in the red shirt took a step closer, his hand still out. Tom flung the cable at him and the end of it caught him on the chest and made a thudding sound. The man stepped back quickly, then looked down at the dirty smudge the cable had made on his shirt, frowned, and started again for Tom. From two steps away, the guy in the blue shirt came at Tom, too.

Tom wound the cable up again with a toss of his right arm and flung it at the two men's faces. It narrowly missed them. They jumped back and Tom swung it again, catching the guy with the blue shirt on his left side. The other tried to tackle

Tom, but landed near the sewer and Tom switched his cable from his right hand to his left. With his right he gave the guy at his feet as hard a blow to the jaw as he'd ever tossed out. The goon fell backward and Tom pushed the garbage can filled with sewer water onto him. While he was busy scrambling away from that, Tom swung his cable back into his right hand and flung it at the guy in the red shirt who began approaching him again.

The cable missed him, but in another instant, Ed Mrazek was outside of the house again, swinging a shovel. He beaned the guy in the red shirt over the head with such force that he knocked the goon on his face in the sewer muck.

A police siren wailed in the distance and the two goons heard it. They got to their feet and gave up on Tom to make a run for their car. Tom was disappointed that the goons drove off up the alley just as a squad car pulled up out front of the house.

Tom dropped the cable and reached out and shook Mrazek's hand. "Nice going!" he said. "Where did you learn to use a shovel like that?"

"I used to work on the railroads," the old man said with pride. "A long time ago. I've been in my share of brawls before. What was that one all about?"

Tom waited until the cops were in the yard, then unloaded his story about Mabley and Costello. The cops said they weren't far away, alerted to patrol the area because the two goons were seen cruising through it. They were hired musclemen and both were wanted on a half-dozen charges. A general call was already in to go after them.

Tom sighed as he went back to work after the cops left. That was the end of round one. When would round two start? He didn't know. But he felt better knowing that Ed Mrazek was in his corner. And not with a towel, but a shovel.

• • •

That night, when he and Jimmy visited Jeff in the hospital, they found Jeff's father at his bedside. A shorter, thinner man than Tom expected, he had an unhealthy red face and seemed very nervous. He needed a drink, Tom figured.

The man said almost nothing to Jeff or to anyone, Tom noticed. *He sure was tight-lipped*, Tom thought. He just wouldn't open up to his son and say what was on his mind.

"Dad wants me to come back home with him tonight," Jeff told his friends. "I'm strong enough, because I can leave here tomorrow. But I'd rather put in with you guys, if it's still okay."

Tom assured Jeff it was still on for him to join the Guardians. He told Jeff's father about the gang and he didn't seem to listen or understand, yet he didn't try to talk Jeff into changing his mind.

They left Jeff and his father alone and checked on Karen. Marty and Ellie had been seeing her as often as they could and they were with her when Tom and Jimmy arrived at her room. Karen had agreed, though reluctantly, to move in with the girls. She didn't put into words what they suspected, that she'd much rather go back to living with Jeff. But everyone but Karen agreed that this arrangement would be best, for both her and Jeff.

Time and again, Tom and Marty tried to find out who her parents were, so they could be notified about her being so sick, but she kept refusing to give her real name or tell them how they could contact her parents. Paul Maggiore told Tom he would work on identifying Karen so her parents could be located, but meanwhile agreed that maybe the best thing for her was to move in again with Marty and Ellie who could take care of her.

Jeff's father was still in his son's room when Tom and Jimmy left that evening. He wasn't there the next morning when they returned to take Jeff home with them. Jeff said his

THE FINAL ACT

father had gone back to Colorado and had given him a little money to help him with living expenses. Jeff told Tom he could have it.

Scotty stayed in the car parked in the hospital garage, to make sure nobody tampered with it. Tom stopped at a supermarket on the way home and bought some sirloin steak on sale, and baking potatoes, to make Jeff's first dinner there something special. Then he drove to Jeff's apartment building and talked to the custodian. Jeff's rent was paid up for the month so there was no problem in his leaving, since he hadn't had a lease. Tom and Jimmy helped Jeff collect his and Karen's things and they took it all to the car and went home.

That night, after they ate, Jeff began unloading his mind on Tom and Jimmy. It was what Tom had been encouraging Jeff to do for days. They sat on the mattress on the floor in the room Jeff would share with Maury and Scotty and talked while the younger members of the gang watched television in the living room.

"You must be wondering what got me in the hospital," Jeff said. "It was so many things, I can hardly remember them all. It was being alone. It was worrying about Mabley and Costello being after me. It was thinking about the drugs I was delivering—not so much worrying I'd get caught, but what it was doing to the kids I was taking it to. And it was mostly kids, around schools. I don't know how I ever did it the first time, much less kept doing it."

Tom understood. He knew Jeff did, too. You do some things you're not proud of, so you can eat. But after a while, it sticks in your gut and you can't do it anymore.

"I had lots of stuff on me all the time," Jeff continued. "It was easy to take some myself." He nervously ran a hand through his hair, then half-laughed. "I think it was mostly Karen. God, she was sure coming on strong. I knew she'd been dumped by some guy named Floyd. She talked about him all the time, and some girl, Betty, he'd taken up with. I knew I was a substitute, but at first, it didn't matter. I was so lonely, I liked it when she turned all her attention onto me. She'd been hired to deal too, by Mabley. That's how I met her. We hit it off and she asked if she could move in with me, since she'd left where she'd been living. Now I know that was with Marty and Ellie."

Tom had an idea that Karen must have had a lot to do with how depressed and desperate Jeff had become.

"The funny thing is," Jeff went on, "I think she really began falling for me. But in the back of her mind she was still so hurt about Floyd dumping her. She told me she started losing weight because she thought she'd be more attractive to Floyd. Then she couldn't stop herself. She thought she'd be able to keep him, and later, when he ran out on her, be able to get him back, if she got really thin. Before she knew it, she'd lost her appetite for food and could hardly stand eating. But then she'd get this wild hunger inside her at times and she'd eat and eat. Then she'd be scared she'd put pounds back on, so she'd make herself throw up."

"It's called bulimia," Tom said. "But then the girl goes right back to starving herself."

Jeff said that was how it was with Karen. "That was bad enough, living with her while she was wasting away starving herself, or stuffing herself with food and vomiting. But she began talking about us like we were already going to set the date and send out the wedding invitations. I told her to hold off, I wasn't ready to get that serious. She got the idea I was about to dump her then, just like Floyd had. I talked and did all I could, but couldn't convince her that I cared for her a lot, and wouldn't leave her. But all she could think of was that I was going to treat her just like Floyd did."

Tom slammed his fist into his palm. "I'd like to meet Floyd sometime."

"She insisted she wasn't talking marriage, that we were both still too young for that," Jeff said. "She just wanted us to 'commit' ourselves to each other. That's how she kept putting it. Well, I couldn't really do that, even though I told her I liked her a lot. I found out pretty fast, how it must be to love somebody and they don't return it, at least as much as the person giving it. I used to laugh about stuff like that. On the soaps they call it 'unrequited love,' I think."

Tom had never experienced it himself, but he thought he could understand and sympathize with Karen. She had loved Floyd very much, or thought she had. He walked out on her and she nearly freaked out, from not having her love for him returned. Then she met Jeff and Tom could see how Karen or any girl could fall hard for him, with his looks and easy manner. First she transferred her unrequited love onto Jeff, then really fell hard for him. But she moved too fast, and too heavy. She scared Jeff, the way any guy might get scared, having a girl fall so hard for him so fast.

"I told her I liked her a lot, but to slow down a little, to let me catch up to her," Jeff said. "I felt kind of overwhelmed. Why was I so special to her, and so fast? Was it just because she needed someone to take Floyd's place, or did she really like me that much?"

Jeff said it went on like that for a couple of weeks, with Karen wanting them to become more serious and he trying to get her to relax and slow down about them.

"Finally, everything seemed to come down on me at once," Jeff told Tom and Jimmy. "Mabley's and Costello's guys were watching every move I made. If I tried quitting them again, I was sure I'd be bumped off. It got so bad I was afraid to leave the apartment, so I didn't. I stayed up there and hid out, but that wasn't any good either, because Karen just stayed around all the time then, and kept pressuring me. I was scared and lonely, so lots of times I let her have her way, just to get her to relax. We had some good times, but there were just too many bad ones, and too much pressure from her. I warned her she would spoil it between us, wanting so much, but that only scared her more and she figured I'd run out on her like Floyd did."

Jeff stopped talking and Tom could see how difficult it was for him to unload all that, but he also could tell that Jeff was glad he was sharing it with them.

"The other night, it just all got to be too much for me," Jeff said after a while. "I had some stuff to deliver and decided to just take it myself. I didn't even know what it was and didn't care. I didn't intend to kill myself with an overdose of anything. I just wanted to shut my eyes and my ears and my head from everything for a while. Maybe when I woke up again, things would be easier to handle, or all my troubles might have gone away. So I swallowed a handful of downers and went to sleep. But when I woke up, wow! Nothing had gone away and I'd just made things worse by blacking out, and I scared Karen so much, she swallowed the stuff I'd left."

They had looked like Romeo and Juliet, Tom thought, now that he heard the full story of how he had come to find them in Jeff's apartment, both close to death.

Jeff was almost shaking, he was so emotionally exhausted after talking about it all. Tom told him to save any more for later, if Jeff wanted to talk more. He got up and left the bedroom. He found a bottle of Catawba in the kitchen and filled a glass and brought it to Jeff. Jeff said it was just what he needed.

"I almost told my father last night that I'd go back to Colorado with him," Jeff said after taking a swallow of the fruit wine. "It would be the easy way out of everything, I thought. Maybe I could escape Mabley and Costello, and Karen, too. But I didn't want to do that to her. I really do like her a lot. If she gave me a little time, maybe I could get as serious about her as she is about me. So I decided the best thing to do was to stick around here. If I left her and went back to Colorado, she might freak out again, and I don't want to have that on my conscience."

Karen probably would go for the final act then, Tom figured. She would feel so rejected, she wouldn't care.

"Heck, I don't want to get serious with anybody," Jeff said, finishing his wine. He lay on his back on the mattress and looked up at Tom and Jimmy. "I've hardly had any fun yet. I figure I've got a lot of beer to drink and ball to play with you guys, before I think of settling down."

Tom laughed. He knew where Jeff was coming from. It was too soon to get tied down to any one girl. And Jeff hadn't had his fun in the sun yet, just horsing around with a bunch of guys. If a guy didn't get that in when he could, he'd never get it in later.

Tom nodded to Jimmy when he saw Jeff close his eyes. They left Jeff alone so he could get some rest. Before leaving his room, Tom looked at Jeff and smiled. He liked the guy. He liked him for not running away from his troubles, and for not dumping Karen. And he liked him for wanting to have his time to do the things guys did. *Jeff and Karen might make it together yet*, he thought. At least, he was more certain now, Jeff would make it.

17

A week after Karen was admitted to the hospital, doctors decided she was well enough to leave. But they prescribed both medication and a diet.

Marty thought it might be easier for Karen if neither Jeff nor Tom were there when she left the hospital. Ellie helped Marty with the girl and they took her right to their apartment. Jeff called Karen later and she told him she'd be okay.

It was going to be a long, rough road ahead for Karen, they all knew. She not only had to recover from the drug overdose, she had to turn her thinking around about starving herself and accept the doctor's diet plan for her. On top of that, and perhaps the hardest thing of all she had to do, she had to try to rebuild her self-image. She had to forget about Floyd and also face the fact that although Jeff liked her a lot, he didn't love her. At least, she knew now, he didn't love her as much as she loved him. Or, she began wondering but not saying, was her love for him just making up for not having Floyd or maybe even just a dependence? Was she just leaning on Jeff because to face life without someone to love her back as much as she needed to be loved was so awful and unacceptable to her, she couldn't handle it?

She hadn't tried to get close to Marty or Ellie before. Now that she moved in with them for a second time, she tried. She saw how easy they were making it for her to just settle in and forget everything that had happened and get on with her main job of getting well again and getting her head and heart together. They didn't have to talk about it. Karen just felt their friendship and support and that, above anything else, began giving her the strength and courage she so desperately needed.

Some good old-fashioned girl talk didn't hurt. Marty and Ellie talked enough about guys and dating and feelings and one-sided love affairs to feed some new thoughts to Karen. They didn't put Floyd or Jeff down; they just casually presented their sides now and then, saying that lots of guys probably mature slower than girls and don't want to get serious or settle down as fast as most girls. Like Jeff, they need more time to play ball with their male friends and to burn rubber in their cars and to flirt with girls and just to be boys. Any heavy pressure to rush them into being men, and to take on all the responsibilities that brings, can scare them off.

"Guys," Ellie suggested during one girl-talk session, "are sort of like mules. You can't rush them, if they don't want to go. Maybe you can gently lead them, but you sure get nowhere if you get behind them and push."

"Sometimes," Marty put in, "I think they're like dogs. They like it a lot better if they're kept on a longer leash."

Karen felt better, hearing them kid about guys. She had her own idea of what kind of animals they were. "I think they're skunks!" she said, then laughed.

It was a good sign, her roommates thought. If she could

THE FINAL ACT

laugh about her guy troubles, she was on her way to knowing how to handle boys better. She would learn, Marty assured her. Ellie added that knowing how to handle a man was a tough job.

Tom found Jeff a bicycle and he joined them on lakefront rides, which helped bring back the healthy Colorado-boy look. When Tom thought Jeff had his feet under himself again, he took him to the gym and introduced him to the boxing coach and his other friends at Turner Park.

Jeff said he'd done a little fighting behind his father's barn at times, but didn't know anything about boxing. When he watched Tom and Jimmy sparring in the ring in their boxing gloves and trunks, he became more interested. Tom suggested that Jeff try his hand at sparring with him awhile. Johnny Lynch thought Jeff ought to work out for a while and punch the bag and learn some of the fundamentals first. Tom and Jimmy volunteered to teach him.

The friends fell into an easy routine. It involved spending every spare hour any of them had each day or evening working out together at the gym. Tom figured nothing could be better for Jeff than the healthy routine they developed, jogging together, skipping rope, punching the bag, sparring, and exercising. Tom hadn't been prepared for what he soon began to discover, watching Jeff during his workouts and sparring. Jeff could become a terrific boxer, if he wanted. He could probably become the best fighter in the gym. Even better, Tom had to admit, than himself.

Tom and Jimmy continued working as volunteers at the suicide prevention center, mainly filling in for others when they had to change their shifts. Tom didn't even suggest that Jeff get in on being a volunteer. He didn't need to hear about any more downers. What Jeff needed was to keep busy and concentrate on boxing and take his mind off everything that had been pulling him down.

Tom became more convinced of how good a fighter Jeff could be when, a week after he brought him to the gym, they got into the ring together for a go at three rounds. They weighed almost the same, Tom being only two pounds heavier. Jimmy stood behind Tom in his corner, while the black trainer, Mike, massaged Jeff.

They came out to center ring and touched gloves and Johnny Lynch, the referee, told them to start boxing. Jeff had learned quickly, Tom realized. He had a good left-right combination and he knew how to duck from the punches Tom threw at him.

Jeff was businesslike in the ring. Friendship was put on hold as soon as the bell clanged. He wasn't an angry fighter and didn't fight dirty, but Tom wasn't his friend as they boxed, he was Jeff's opponent, as it should be. When Tom finally realized that halfway through the first round, when Jeff's blows had staggered him a few times, he played the rest of the bout by Jeff's rules. He gave as good as Jeff gave.

Jimmy and Mike looked across the ring at each other near the end of the first round and smiled. It was one of the best matches they'd seen at the gym or even in the Golden Gloves. *Too bad*, Jimmy was thinking, *Tom and Jeff were in the same boxing club*. They wouldn't get to put on a show like this in public and would be paired against other fighters from other clubs. What a title match they would put on, if they were from opposing gyms.

When Jimmy massaged Tom in his corner after the bell sounded, he told Tom he thought the round ended even.

"Work on his midsection," Jimmy advised. "I don't think he has the knockout punch he thinks he has. Go for it on points. Unless you think you can TKO him."

THE FINAL ACT

Tom nearly laughed, though his shoulder hurt a little from one blow Jeff had landed. "I don't think I can kayo him!"

During round two, a left jab of Jeff's came out of nowhere and landed hard on Tom's chin, sending him bouncing on the canvas on his rear end. He shook the surprise out of his head, got up at the count of six, and decided the fooling around was over. If he'd been holding back until then, because Jeff was his friend, he wouldn't hold back anymore. He'd go for it.

Tom came back with enough lefts and rights to send Jeff crouching back against the ropes and Johnny Lynch separated them. They went at it toe to toe for another minute until the bell clanged again.

Jeff stood up in his corner while Mike rubbed his legs and talked to him. Tom sat on his stool and felt more tired than he ever had in a fight before. Jimmy helped him take deep breaths by lifting his waistband out and massaging his chest.

A good-size crowd of spectators gathered to watch the bout at ringside. Tom was tired but felt good. He'd never been in a scrap like this and felt up for it. He looked at Jeff across the ring just before the bell sounded again for the final round, and caught a look on Jeff's face that made him feel good. Jeff was going to give his best, but the look told Tom that it was still just between friends.

They touched gloves again at the start of the third round, then went at it like never before. Jimmy could see that even Johnny Lynch was impressed with both of his boys. It was a good, hard, clean fight. He almost never had to break them because they rarely went into a clinch. Not a low blow was thrown by either fighter. Jeff had learned the rules not only of good boxing but of smart boxing as well, and he had learned them fast. What it was telling not only those watching from outside the ring and Lynch in the ring, but Tom himself, was that Jeff was showing signs of being a natural-born boxer.

It was okay, Tom had thought in his corner before the third round. A distance runner did his best when the competition was keenest. It was the same in the ring, he figured. The better your opponent was, the better you had to put out. And Tom knew, during the final round, that at least he was putting out his best. The only thing that he wondered about was, was Jeff really doing his best or was he still holding back a little?

That question got answered in the final minute of the round. Tom had exchanged punches pretty evenly with Jeff until one right caught him on the side of the head. Tom went sprawling back against the ropes and nearly fell through them. He rested on the ropes for another six-count while Lynch sent Jeff to a neutral corner.

Catching his breath as he stood against the ropes for the count, Tom saw Jeff dancing anxiously in his corner, getting ready to come at him again. The look Jeff had on his face in his corner between rounds was gone. This was just one boxer against another now. Well, that was how it ought to be, Tom decided as he came away from the ropes at the count of six, and he and Jeff went at it again.

A barrage of lefts and rights from Jeff to Tom's midsection ended when Tom was able to land a solid right to Jeff's chin. It sent Jeff tumbling backward this time and he landed on his rear end with a thump. The bell sounded and Lynch called the fight over.

Both fighters rested in their corners while their handlers toweled them off and took off their gloves and took out their mouthpieces. There had been no team of judges at ringside. The referee's decision would judge the fight.

After a few minutes, Lynch motioned for the boxers to come to the middle of the ring. He looked at Jeff, then at Tom, then lifted both their hands.

"A draw, or I'm the Easter bunny!"

It was a good decision, Tom thought, moving past the coach and embracing Jeff. But he still wondered, as Jeff hugged him back, if Jeff hadn't been holding back, maybe just a little.

18

Driving back to the loft after the fight that Friday night, Tom was at the wheel of the old Volkswagen with Jimmy beside him and Jeff in the back seat. Halfway home, they were startled by an explosion from somewhere beneath the car.

Tom pulled over to a curb and they all smelled a lot of gas fumes in the car, even though the windows were open. Tom told his friends to get away from the car, in case it was going to blow up. Cautiously, from a little distance, Tom looked the car over. It didn't take him long to realize what had happened.

"The muffler must have blown," he called out to Jimmy and Jeff. "The tail pipes fell off. It's okay," he said, waving for them to come back to the car. "Nobody tampered with it. I was expecting muffler trouble. The car was starting to sound like a jet plane about to take off."

Tom told Jeff about all the trouble he'd been having since he bought Paul Maggiore's old car. Paul had warned him it needed a lot of work, but Tom was just discovering how much that was. Jeff couldn't help but laugh when Jimmy told about how the floor under the driver's seat had given way a few weeks before and Tom had nearly fallen through to the street.

The car could still be driven home, but they rolled the windows all the way down so they could breathe with all the gas fumes coming up at them. Tom got them home, then put off repairing the car until the next day.

It was getting to be a little discouraging, Tom thought, mentally adding up all the time and money he'd been spending to repair the car lately. But he had no choice. He couldn't afford to buy a new or even newer used car, yet he could barely afford keeping the old clunker fixed up and running. What he needed was a regular job again, not just the part-time money he got for helping Ed Mrazek a few times a week.

Tom checked again with Paul Maggiore about any possible job he might be able to find for him, but Paul said he was still working on it and hadn't come up with anything yet. Tom said it wasn't just for him, but Jeff and Jimmy needed work, too. Paul said he would keep working on it.

Later that night, they biked over to the girls' apartment. It was the first time Jeff had gone there since Karen moved in with Marty and Ellie about a week before. Though it hadn't been planned, the others went for a ride on their bikes and left Jeff and Karen alone.

Soon as Tom and his friends started biking away from the apartment building, Tom began looking over his shoulder. He didn't know why, but he began feeling especially concerned that they were being followed or watched. He didn't like the feeling and wished they were in his car instead of on bikes.

The night was warm and clear, with a nice breeze blowing in off the lake. They pedaled south into Lincoln Park and headed for the Diversey Harbor. Soon they were pedaling

THE FINAL ACT   145

toward the zoo, with the lagoon to their left, when Tom realized that two cars had pulled up a short way behind them. Looking behind him, he saw four big guys get out. He thought he recognized two of them as the goons who had tried to wipe him out the afternoon he'd been working with Ed Mrazek.

Tom became worried, not for himself but for the girls and Jimmy. He didn't have any weapon on him. They were on bikes and couldn't hope to get away from the thugs if they pursued in their cars. As the four men began to approach them from their parked cars, Tom shouted to his friends.

"Four guys are after us!" he cried. "Let's get out of here!"

He pedaled a little slower than Jimmy and the girls, to let them get ahead of him, then looked behind him again. The four men were running back to their cars.

Tom didn't like it. Biking on the roadway, they were like sitting ducks for the goons to drive them down. Maybe they were better off leaving their bikes and running for it toward the zoo. There were some people around there, none where they were biking. Maybe a crowd would discourage the goons.

They heard the screech of rubber and revving of engines as the two cars sped toward them in the night.

"Leave the bikes!" Tom shouted up to his friends. "Let's make a run for it toward the zoo! Stay off the road!"

Marty and Jimmy pulled their bikes over to the side of the road and jumped off while Tom left his bike a little way behind them. The three of them were safely off the road and starting for some bushes when Tom looked back and saw that his sister had lost control of her bike and was still trying to get off, when the two cars were nearly on top of her.

There was a crunching sound, a scream, and the cars sped on up the road, heading north again up Cannon Drive. Tom didn't see Ellie at first in the darkness, then heard her calling his name. Leaving the bushes, Tom, Jimmy, and Marty ran along the roadway until they found Ellie. She was lying alongside the road. Beside her, her bicycle lay in a tangled, mangled mess.

She was more frightened than hurt, they discovered. Her left ankle hurt, she had bruises on her arms and legs, but she assured them she hadn't been seriously injured. But when she tried to stand, she found she couldn't because of a sprained ankle.

Tom looked ahead and saw the two cars enter the traffic that led out of the park and into the city. He was glad to see the goons hadn't decided to circle back and come after them again to try for a second chance at running them down.

They all knew who had sent the goons after them and Tom thought he'd had about enough of Mabley and Costello and their musclemen. Soon as he could get his car fixed, he'd go out after them and settle things once and for all. It was bad enough they were after him, he didn't want them going after the girls or Jimmy again.

Jimmy walked both his bike and Tom's while Tom helped his sister walk to where some cars and people were, nearby at the zoo. He found a waiting taxi and had enough money to pay for the driver to take Ellie to her apartment. He and Jimmy and Marty would meet her there on their bikes.

When they were all together again back at the girls' place, Tom and Jimmy helped Ellie upstairs. Jeff was still there with Karen and Tom told them what had happened at the lakefront. He could see that Jeff looked relieved that they had come back. *Jeff needed rescuing*, Tom thought. Karen looked unhappy, but Tom sort of expected that. Whatever they had talked about, Tom figured it wasn't going to make Karen very happy. Jeff had told him earlier that he hoped to explain things to Karen, to talk her into going slower where

THE FINAL ACT

they were concerned. But Tom sensed that Karen was at least trying to handle it. She didn't look desperate or like she might come unglued, though he had seen a lot of girls look a lot happier.

Tom collapsed in an easy chair in the girls' living room after they'd helped Ellie by applying ice to her ankle. *What next?* he wondered.

19

The next thing happened fast. Ellie's sprained ankle began to swell up and give her great pain.

Tom couldn't remember feeling so frustrated. He'd have to call another taxi to take his sister to the hospital. His car was sick again and falling apart. He had to borrow cab fare from Marty because he was down to loose pocket change.

He just *had* to get a steady job and some money, to get the car fixed up so it would be dependable, and to afford things like cab fares in emergencies.

Marty, of course, didn't mind putting up money for the cab fare. What worried them all was how were they going to pay the hospital bill? Jeff's father had paid for his hospital stay, but officials there were still trying to figure out how to get paid for Karen's treatment.

Tom and Marty took Ellie to the hospital by taxi while Jeff and Jimmy bicycled home and Tom left his bike at Marty's. Karen told them she'd be all right alone there until Marty and Ellie got back.

Ellie was treated at the emergency room at Grant Hospital

and Tom and Marty waited in the visitors' lounge for nearly two hours. It finally developed that Ellie's fall was more serious than first believed. She'd torn some ligaments in her ankle and the leg had to be put in a cast. After two hours, she greeted them from a wheel chair, with a crutch across her lap.

Tom wheeled her to a waiting taxi and helped her into the passenger seat beside the driver, then got in back with Marty. Afterward, when Ellie was back at her place and resting, Tom got his bike and pedaled away from the apartment building. By then it was nearly two o'clock in the morning and he looked behind him anxiously every few minutes as he biked home.

To his relief, he made it home without incident. He half-expected someone to appear out of nowhere, on foot or in cars, and come down on him since he was alone. *How much longer was it going to go on?* he wondered. He was tired of it all, tired of living in fear, not only for himself but for his sister and Marty and the guys. It was obvious to him now that if the musclemen didn't go after him, they'd take it out on the others. How was he going to keep something terrible from happening to them?

He remembered Larry Schroeder and his dream of escaping everything and going out to California. It was a thought that began coming back to Tom lately. He didn't like to think it would mean he was running away. He'd take everybody with him. They could all get a fresh start out on the West Coast. He hated Chicago winters anyway. It was late spring then, but before long it would be cold again, as it always seemed to be to him.

A fresh start sounded so good, so hopeful. Maybe he could shake Mabley and Costello off if he and his friends split. They wouldn't have to live in fear anymore. They could get jobs out in California doing anything and it would be okay. It was cheaper to live out there, he'd heard. You didn't have to pay heating bills, anyway. He had a vague picture of orange trees off of which you could pick fruit for free. At least, even if they were broke, they'd never starve.

He lay awake on top of his mattress in his room with Jimmy, both of them just in boxer shorts because the morning was warm and humid and only a slight breeze blew the curtains on the one window in their room. He couldn't sleep. Too much was on his mind.

He was about as broke as he'd ever been in his life, and Ed Mrazek's back had begun bothering him, so he accepted fewer sewer rodding jobs. That meant he called Tom less frequently and that resulted in less money in Tom's pocket. Jeff and Jimmy kept trying as he had to find work, but they all met with blank walls. There didn't seem to be any jobs anywhere.

Tom couldn't sleep, long after he saw that Jimmy had dropped off. He got up and walked into the living room and found Jeff there, watching television with the sound off. He sat in just his shorts and Tom plopped down next to him on the couch.

"You couldn't sleep either?" Tom said softly. He saw that there was an old John Wayne western on the tube, *Red River*, with Montgomery Clift and a great cast, about the first big cattle drive out West in the late 1800s. He knew what was happening even with the sound off. He practically knew all the actors' lines by heart, but it still seemed strange watching the picture as if it were a silent movie. He thought Jeff was very considerate, to turn the sound off so it wouldn't wake the other guys up.

"Karen," Jeff replied. "We talked while you guys were out on your bikes. She kept trying to put pressure on me again. I almost had too much and told her to quit it or I wouldn't call her or come around anymore. I didn't want to do that. She might try something stupid again, like we both did."

Tom looked at Jeff with concern.

"Don't worry," Jeff told him. "I won't do that again. I just hope Karen won't. But I'm just about ready to call it quits with her. I've just about had it. I told her how I don't want to get heavy with her or with any girl right now. I swear, Tom, I think girls have only one thing on their minds, to land a guy they set their sights on. Everybody used to say that guys were the ones who were after the girls, but I'll tell you, I think it's the other way around now."

Tom thought it was almost funny but didn't laugh. Here Jeff was complaining that Karen was pressuring him to get more serious, and it *was* the other way around with him and Marty. Marty kept telling Tom to cool it and go slower and let them have a chance to grow up and get their life's dreams started. Tom was having a hard time handling his feelings for Marty. He could imagine how it was for Karen, feeling so strongly for Jeff but seeing how more casual Jeff wanted their relationship to be.

Was it unrequited love? Tom wondered. Maybe it was even unrequited friendship. He remembered how the crazy teenager, Angel, had been so devoted to their friend Larry. But Larry just held Angel off and let him be a more casual friend. Only now could Tom come close to appreciating the disappointment or rejection Angel must have felt. To Angel, Larry was a very special person, but to Larry, Angel was just another person in his life.

Tom felt certain he was more than just another person in Marty's life, no matter how things would work out between them. He seemed less certain about Jeff and Karen that morning as Jeff talked more about his problem with Karen.

"Sometimes, I think maybe I ought to go back and live

THE FINAL ACT 153

with my father," Jeff said after a while, getting up and starting back for his room.

"Hang on a while," Tom urged him, putting a hand on his shoulder. "We're both too tired to think straight."

What they all needed was a weekend away from the city, Tom decided when he got back in bed. Soon as Ellie's ankle healed and she could ride her bike again, they would all get on their bikes and take a trip to Indiana or Michigan, like he'd been wanting. The thought of that relaxed him and he finally fell asleep.

The telephone awakened him the next morning. Marty called to say that Karen had split again.

"She took her things and left sometime before I got up this morning," Marty said. "She left a short note, thanking us all for trying to help her. She didn't leave any clue as to where she was going. Did Jeff tell you anything? Did they have a lovers' quarrel?"

Tom explained briefly that Jeff felt very pressured again. "He didn't exactly say that they quarreled. I don't really think he sees himself as her lover, or she his. What I think is, she still hasn't gotten over Floyd."

Marty sighed. "I don't know what to do. I don't suppose there's anything any of us can do. We never did learn who her parents are, or where they live. We don't know who to call about her."

Tom said that Paul Maggiore was still working on that, but hadn't come up with anything yet. But Tom did have one thought, or fear.

"She may have gone over to Mabley or Costello again," he said, thinking aloud. "She was delivering drugs for them before. She probably needs money. That'd be the quickest way for her to get some. I'll tell Paul and maybe he can check that angle out."

Later, when Jeff woke up, Tom laid the news on him and

Jeff began to worry about Karen more than ever. Tom could see how guilt-ridden Jeff felt, and tried to talk him out of feeling responsible for Karen. Jeff got dressed, skipped breakfast, and said he would take his bike and cruise the neighborhoods, hoping to find Karen.

Tom spent the rest of the day working as fast as he could on his car to get it serviceable again. Jimmy knew next to nothing about cars, but stuck with Tom and did what he could until the job was done later that night. Some spare parts from an auto graveyard Tom knew did the trick and Tom installed a muffler and tail pipes that weren't brand new, but came off a newer car than his that had been in a wreck.

After dinner, Tom and Jimmy got in the car and started driving around, looking for Jeff as well as Karen. Jeff hadn't come back since he left that morning. Tom wished he'd at least have phoned. As the hours went by, he became more anxious about both of them.

It was a hot May night, so humid that Tom's black nylon shirt stuck to him. *Maybe it was because of the weather,* he thought, or maybe it was because he was so anxious. As they cruised around, he didn't see the plainclothes cop, Wes Roeder. He didn't see anyone else he thought looked like a cop hanging around to look out for him. Maybe, he figured, Roeder had the night off and the watch commander was short on men and didn't put a relief man on.

It didn't matter that much to Tom. He hadn't expected anyone to fight his battles for him at any time before in his life. He sure didn't expect it now.

But Tom worried about Jimmy. He didn't want him hurt, if anything happened. He told him he'd rather drop him off back at the warehouse. Jimmy looked at Tom as if he were crazy and wouldn't even humor him by arguing about it.

They kept cruising until nearly one in the morning. People were still out in front of their houses, leaning out of windows, or hanging around on street corners. It was too hot and muggy to go to bed and everyone was trying to catch a breath of fresh air but there wasn't any. Tom thought the city felt like one big steambath.

Driving west up Fullerton Avenue not far from the Diversey Harbor and lagoon in Lincoln Park, Tom saw a car pass his that had a driver who looked familiar to him. He became certain it was one of the two musclemen who had come after him that day when he had been working on the sewer. Maybe the guy riding with him was the other goon.

Tom followed the car as it turned off Fullerton and drove north onto Geneva Terrace. When it stopped in front of an old brownstone building, Tom pulled his Volkswagen to the curb half a block away and turned off the lights and ignition. When the two giants got out of their car, he was more certain they were the two guys Mabley and Costello had sent after him. But what interested Tom more was the car he saw parked in front of the three-story brownstone. Light from a nearby lamppost reflected off the silver Audi and it stood there fairly glowing.

The two men got out of their car and started for the brownstone. One of them carried a small suitcase. They paused for a moment in front of the Audi. Then they went up some stone stairs to a big red door, opened it, and went into a small vestibule, then closed the door behind them.

After the men were out of sight, Tom and Jimmy approached the building. They walked up a narrow gangway close to another building that looked like a clone of the one the goons had gone into. When they came into a small backyard behind the building, Tom saw a bicycle propped against some garbage cans. He looked it over and decided he recognized it. It didn't have a fender over the rear wheel.

"I'm positive it's Jeff's," Tom told Jimmy. "He must have spotted Mabley or Costello, or maybe Karen. Nobody would have let him ride his bike here. He must have come without anyone knowing, then got caught. I bet he's inside right now. Let's look around some more."

They saw lights on in the first-floor windows, but not in the basement or on the second or third floors. *It was a big, old house that could sleep a lot of people,* Tom thought. It would make a great gang hideout.

There was no easy way to see inside any of the lighted windows. Tom walked along the other side of the building, up another gangway close to another identical house, looking for something to stand on so he could hoist himself up and look inside one of the windows.

Near the front of the gangway, he saw a small iron railing around a flight of stone stairs that led down to the basement of the house next door. He climbed on top of the railing, leaned forward against the brownstone, and looked into a small window.

It was a bathroom, Tom discovered. The door inside was open but the room was not occupied. He didn't see anyone through the door, which he saw opened onto a hallway.

Tom waited several anxious minutes, then saw someone pass through the hall from the back to the front of the house. He saw the man for only a moment, but there was no mistaking him. He jumped down from the railing and took his car keys out of his jeans pocket.

"Here, Jim-boy," Tom said, handing him the keys, "I just saw Costello inside. I bet it's a drug buy. I didn't see Jeff, but I figure he's inside somewhere. I'll stick around here. You go for the cops."

Jimmy tried to talk Tom into going for the police with him, but Tom said it was better if he stayed there, in case they all left the building. Maybe he could follow them if they split.

Reluctantly, Jimmy took the keys and ran. Tom went back to casing the building, then climbed atop the railing next to

THE FINAL ACT 157

the bathroom. It was the only place he could find from which he could look inside the brownstone.

Just as he began looking inside the building again, Tom was startled by the sound of someone approaching from the gangway in the backyard.

20

"Tom, is that you?" a familiar voice called out in the dark gangway.

Tom squinted and saw that it was Jeff.

"How'd you find this place?" Jeff asked as Tom jumped down from the railing.

Tom and Jeff moved into the backyard and Tom explained how he and Jimmy had gotten there.

"I saw the Audi parked out front," Jeff said. "Karen's inside. I jimmied open the basement door and looked around but couldn't get upstairs. The door leading upstairs must be locked and bolted from the inside. Karen wasn't in the basement. But I saw her pass by the hallway, from the window you were looking in."

"There's some sort of drug deal going on inside," Tom said. "I saw Costello inside. Some of their musclemen just brought a suitcase full of something to them. It could be money or drugs. I just sent Jimmy to bring the cops."

They heard voices out front of the building. Tom cautioned Jeff as he led the way back up the gangway toward the street.

Another sound drew their attention. Tom stopped anxiously and they both listened.

"The house is on fire!" Tom exclaimed.

Looking up, they saw that the lights were turned off in the house, but flames were already lapping up against the windows on the first floor.

They hid in the darkness of the gangway as they approached the front of the building. They saw Mabley and Costello standing on the sidewalk talking with the two goons. At first, they didn't see her, then Karen stepped out from behind Costello. He was holding her by the arm and she didn't look like she wanted to go with them.

Tom wished the cops would get there. In another minute or two, they might be too late. He wondered how he could follow them, if they got into the cars and drove away.

Mabley, he saw, had the suitcase. The two goons were stuffing envelopes into their sportcoat pockets and started for their car. Mabley and Costello started for the Audi, Costello keeping a firm hold on Karen's right arm. She looked frightened and kept trying to free her arm, but Costello wouldn't let her go.

Tom looked at Jeff. "We've got to get Karen," he said, starting to leave the darkness of the gangway.

"They've probably got guns," Jeff warned as he started to follow close behind Tom.

Tom wished he heard police sirens but heard none. There was nothing else they could do but go for it. Flames were coming out the windows of the brownstone by then and the upper floors of the building had caught fire.

Flames began leaping out at Tom and Jeff as they started out of the gangway. Mabley saw them and called to Costello. Surprised, Costello momentarily loosened his grip on Karen's arm. She freed herself and, seeing Tom and Jeff, made a run for them.

THE FINAL ACT

Costello drew a gun out of his coat and fired at Karen. Then he ran for the Audi. Mabley was already in the car and Costello opened the door on the passenger side and got in, then turned in his seat and aimed his gun again at Karen as she was about to reach Tom and Jeff at the entrance to the gangway.

Before Costello could fire again, an explosion shook the ground under Tom and his friends. At first, Tom thought it had come from the burning building. After a moment the smoke cleared a little, and, through a wall of flames, they saw what it was. The Audi had blown up in front of the building, with Mabley and Costello inside.

The two musclemen could be seen walking toward their car. At the sound of the explosion, they looked behind them, stopped, and looked satisfied.

It began to make sense to Tom. The hired goons had double-crossed Mabley and Costello. They'd wired a bomb to go off when the ignition was turned on in the Audi, even though they expected Karen to be in the car with their bosses.

Whatever deal the goons had made, Mabley and Costello got the short end of it. They had paid the goons off for what must have been a deal, but maybe there wasn't anything but bricks in the suitcase that had been taken into the Audi with them. Seeing the Audi turn into a wall of flames, Tom figured that that part of the mystery would never be solved.

"Jeff, let's go for them!" Tom called as he started after the musclemen who began walking toward their car.

Jeff ran after Tom as people began coming out of the buildings on either side of the one on fire and gathered on the sidewalk in their nightclothes. Karen didn't follow Tom and Jeff. She was still too weak and frightened. She moved away from the burning car and building and a woman in a robe came over and put her arm around her.

The goons got in their car before Tom or Jeff could reach

them and the car sped away in a screech of rubber. The friends began running after the car just as they heard the wail of sirens pierce the air. They saw some squad cars approaching, their dome lights blazing and sirens screaming as they pulled into the street and cut the car off. Behind the squad cars Tom saw his old Volkswagen pull over and stop.

A squad car sideswiped the getaway car and it went out of control and crashed into a lamppost. The driver was trapped behind the wheel, but his partner got out of the car and began making a run for it. He tried escaping up a gangway between the cops and Tom and Jeff, but Tom ran up the narrow gangway and tackled the man by the legs.

Together, Tom and Jeff held the man until police took him off their hands. Moments later, the sound of fire engines filled the air and hook and ladder trucks began pulling up near the burning building and car.

Firemen and paramedics tried to get Mabley and Costello out of the Audi, but it was no use. Later, Tom heard that they probably had been killed instantly by the explosion, before they could burn to death.

No one was found inside the building. Gasoline had been spilled throughout the first floor and the fire spread so rapidly, the house went up like a matchbox set afire.

In all the confusion, Tom didn't see Jimmy until he came walking up to him and Jeff and Karen as they stood away from the burning building.

"Everything's all right now," Tom told Jimmy, and his friend could see that they were all safe.

Mabley and Costello had gotten what was coming to them. They couldn't hire kids like Jeff or Karen to do their dirty work anymore. *It was poetic justice,* Tom thought, that they should have been double-crossed by their own hired men, and then gotten blown up in the Audi when they had sent the goons to fix Tom's car so it would explode with him in it. Now police had both of the hired killers in custody and they wouldn't be causing Tom or his friends any more trouble.

Tom almost laughed, from relief and from what he saw around him. It looked like World War III with the Audi still on fire and the brownstone's roof crashing in amid a rush of flames and smoke and intense heat. It was hot enough that early morning, without the fire.

Out of the maze of fire trucks and police cars and paramedic ambulances, Tom saw a familiar face.

He did laugh as he saw a big man come toward him and his friends. He was casually dressed in jeans and pullover shirt and looked very concerned.

Where were you, Tom wondered as he saw Wes Roeder approach, *when we needed you?*

21

Things were not much less eventful in the days that followed. Paul Maggiore had located Karen's folks in Wilmette. They came for her at Marty's and Ellie's apartment and Karen surprised her roommates by being willing to listen to them. They had agreed to divorce, but her mother seemed to want her so badly, and said she was undergoing treatment for her drug problem, that Karen agreed to go home with her.

Karen and Jeff had a chance to talk to each other by themselves after Karen made her decision. Jeff told Tom about it a few days later, on a bike ride they took together.

"We both said we were sorry," Jeff said, "but that maybe this was the best thing for both of us right now. I told her I've made a decision, too."

Tom had been expecting it. He thought he knew what Jeff was going to say, and he was sorry about it.

"I called my dad last night," Jeff told him. "I said I'd take a bus and come back home. I've thought about it a lot lately, especially after he came to see me in the hospital. You know, Tom, I never thought my father really cared about me, whether I lived or died. He was so wrapped up in feeling sorry for himself that my mom split on him. He drank himself into a hole he just crawled into. But when he came all the way here to Chicago to see if I was okay, it started to register on me. He needs me and I guess I need him, too."

They stopped biking along the lakefront on another cooler, starry night, and shook hands.

"I told Karen that when she feels better, she ought to come out to Colorado and I can take her horseback riding," Jeff said, deep in thought as they pedaled farther again, coming to the lagoon at Diversey Harbor.

Tom liked what he heard from Jeff. It was going to be okay for them. Maybe they'd never ever get as serious as Karen hoped they would, but then again, maybe they would. It was up to the two of them to work it out, and that much they had going for them.

It felt safe, riding a bike at night along the lagoon path again. Tom no longer had to look anxiously over his shoulder.

But he had to admit he felt sorry that Jeff was going to leave. He thought he made the right decision, to go back home and live with his father. But he couldn't help thinking how much he'd miss him. He'd grown to like Jeff a lot and to respect him very much. The two went hand-in-glove, Tom realized. He couldn't like someone, or love him, unless he respected him. Jeff had handled himself and Tom had nothing but the highest respect for him.

Tom would also miss their times together in the ring. It made Tom think about the boxing future Jeff probably was giving up.

"If you'd hung around me some more, in boxing trunks and gloves," Tom joked, "you might have become a pretty good fighter."

THE FINAL ACT

"I think from now on, all I may get to do is punch cattle." Jeff laughed. "When we're not planting or plowing, I work on a neighbor's ranch."

Jeff looked like a cowboy on a bike, Tom thought, as his friend rode on a little way ahead of him in his jeans and blue satin western shirt and boots. He was going to miss him. But maybe sometime that summer, he and the others might all climb in the old Volkswagen and drive out to Colorado and check out the farm and look up their friend.

That night, after he and Jimmy saw Jeff off at the Greyhound bus station in the Loop, they drove back to the suicide prevention center and worked two shifts, from eight to midnight, then from midnight to four in the morning.

They volunteered for a double shift that ended that Friday morning because they wanted to have the weekend off. After sleeping until noon, they went out and bought groceries for the weekend for the guys and put them in the refrigerator. Then they checked the air in their bike tires and stuffed some camping gear into a pair of backpacks.

The phone interrupted them and Tom found it was Bernie Schmidt calling with good news. He hurried back outside behind the warehouse where Jimmy was loading their bikes for a trip, and swung his friend around and hugged him.

"Bernie's got a big job and needs us back working for him!" Tom exclaimed. "Starting Monday!"

It would make the weekend bike trip the guys were starting out on with their girls even more special. They biked over to Marty and Ellie's place after the girls got out of school. Ellie's ankle had healed fast and she was riding her bike again with no trouble.

At the girls' apartment, they helped them finish packing and soon were outside on their bikes, pedaling north up the long bike path in Lincoln Park, heading for the north suburbs. They would stop and look in on Karen in Wilmette and see how she was doing, on their way up into Wisconsin for the weekend.

The heat wave had passed, the sky was blue, a cooler and drier air mass had moved down from Canada to push away the tropical humid weather from the Gulf of Mexico, and Tom felt like letting out with a cowboy yell as he biked beside Marty. Jimmy and Ellie pedaled a short way ahead of them on the bike path. A calm, bluish green Lake Michigan lay sleepily to their right.

Tom thought life was pretty good. He'd been waiting for it to take that kind of a turn for a long time.

TOM DELOS AND THE GUARDIANS ADVENTURES

by Walter Oleksy

In a world that keeps dealing nothing but bad breaks, staying out of trouble isn't easy. For Tom Delos, forming the Guardians was his last chance to prove to himself and to others that he could achieve something. From now on, helping kids like himself—loners, down and outers, orphans and kids who needed a second chance —would be his quest.

_____	UP FROM NOWHERE #1	16831-6/$2.25
_____	ONE WAY TRIP #2	13775-5/$1.95
_____	EASY WAY OUT #3	15720-9/$1.95

Available at your local bookstore or return this form to:

TEMPO
Book Mailing Service
P.O. Box 690, Rockville Centre, NY 11571

Please send me the titles checked above. I enclose _____. Include 75¢ for postage and handling if one book is ordered; 25¢ per book for two or more not to exceed $1.75. California, Illinois, New York and Tennessee residents please add sales tax.

NAME_____

ADDRESS_____

CITY_____ STATE/ZIP_____

(allow six weeks for delivery)

T-8

MAGICQUEST

A new fantasy series featuring the best in Young Adult Fantasy— classic titles of magic and adventure by the top authors in the fantasy field, in paperback for the very first time!

THE THROME OF THE ERRIL OF SHERILL
by World Fantasy Award Winner
Patricia A. McKillip _____ 80839-5/$2.25

THE PERILOUS GARD
A Newbery Honor Winner by
Elizabeth Marie Pope _____ 65956-X/$2.25

THE SEVENTH SWAN
by the acclaimed British fantasist
Nicholas Stuart Gray _____ 75955-6/$2.25

THE ASH STAFF
first of the Ash Staff series by
Paul R. Fisher _____ 03115-3/$2.25

Available at your local bookstore or return this form to:

TEMPO
Book Mailing Service
P.O. Box 690, Rockville Centre, NY 11571

Please send me the titles checked above. I enclose _____. Include 75¢ for postage and handling if one book is ordered; 25¢ per book for two or more not to exceed $1.75. California, Illinois, New York and Tennessee residents please add sales tax.

NAME_____

ADDRESS_____

CITY_____STATE/ZIP_____

(allow six weeks for delivery)

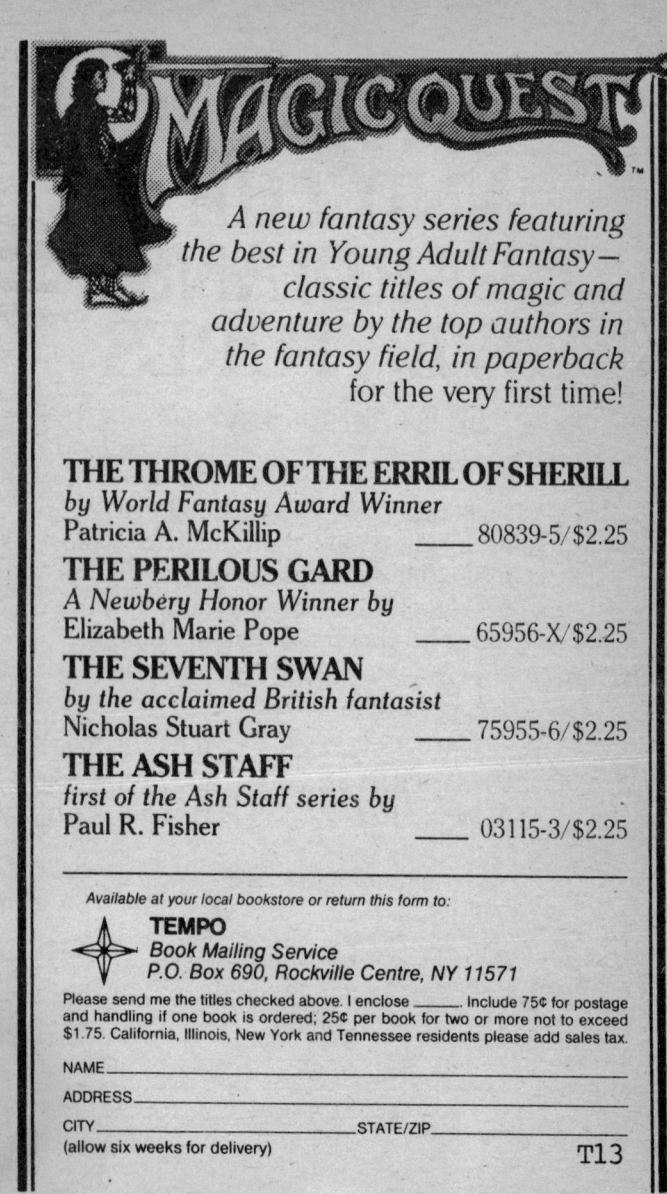

T13